World of Wanda

To those of you with heads full of pesky,
noisy hamster wheels . . . I see you!

World of Wanda is a uclanpublishing book

First published in Great Britain in 2025 by
uclanpublishing
University of Central Lancashire
Preston, PR1 2HE, UK

Text copyright © Karen McCombie 2025
Cover illustration by Stephanie Jade Howe

978-1-916747-46-3

1 3 5 7 9 10 8 6 4 2

The right of Karen McCombie and Stephanie Jade Howe to be identified
as the author and illustrator of this work respectively has been asserted
in accordance with the Copyright, Designs and Patents Act 1988.

All rights reserved. No part of this publication may be reproduced,
stored in a retrieval system, or transmitted in any form or by any means,
electronic, mechanical, photocopying, recording or otherwise,
without the prior permission of the publishers.

Set in 11/16.5pt Museo 100 by Amy Cooper

A CIP catalogue record for this book is available from the British Library.
Printed and bound in Great Britain by Clays Ltd, Elcograf S.p.A.

uclanpublishing

World of Wanda

KAREN McCOMBIE

SEPTEMBER

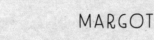

MARGOT

Dear Diary,

Help! My chest feels like there's a bunch of bats flapping around in there.

And right now, I'm sitting on my bed, knowing I should be getting ready, knowing I should be picking up my bag and heading downstairs. But I just need to scribble some stuff down, in case it helps with the bat attack.

The thing is, today's the first day back at school after the summer holidays. It'll be the first time I'll have seen Marisa since she resigned from being my best friend. Awkward. Also, I keep thinking about how totally hyper everyone's going to be. The playground will be mobbed, with everyone squealing their hellos and hugging and madly catching up.

If – I mean, when – I get asked how my summer's been, I don't know how I can even begin to explain what's gone on with me. There was the Marisa stuff, obviously. But even though that felt huge and hurtful at the time, what happened next just . . . well, it just eclipsed it. Cos exactly six weeks ago, something mind-melting happened to my family. Or I guess I should say someone happened to us.

Before that, it was like me and my parents and my little brother Charlie were packed together in this neat little snow globe, just the four of us staring out of the shiny clear plastic. Then The Someone appeared on our doorstep, with no warning.

The Someone who smiled this gap-toothed smile at us all and then grabbed our family snow globe and shook it till me and Mum and Dad and Charlie were lost in a total blizzard. That's what it felt like.

And that's what I've got to tell people about today. That our family of four is – surprise, surprise – actually a family of five.

That all this time I had – drum roll, please! – a secret sister.

A SECRET SISTER!!!

Okay, so Mum's shouting my name. She's shouting Wanda's too.

#HereGoes

#WishMeLuck

SIX WEEKS
EARLIER

THURSDAY

WANDA

'Hola, mi llamo Wanda!'

I scratch the words in the dry earth with the end of the small wooden spoon I just ate my yoghurt with.

'Hej, mitt namn är Wanda!'

An ant is walking over the 'Hej'.

Why is it on its own? Where are its ant buddies? Don't they hang out in colonies? How many ants are in a colony, anyway? Hundreds? Thousands? Hundreds of thousands? I wonder if that little ant is lonely. Or maybe it just got bored of doing ant stuff and came to watch what the Big Human (me) was doing . . .

'สวัสดีฉันชื่อ Wanda!'

Actually, I don't know about the ant, but *I'm* kind

of bored. Like itchy-in-my-skin bored. My mum Patti and all the other grown-ups are either still working in the fields or taking a lunch break in the shade somewhere on the farm cos it's so, so, SO hot.

"Huh? What are you saying, Wanda?" asks Elif, from the stripy hammock swinging between two gnarly trees in the scrubby garden. She's made the hammock *her* territory; the other adults don't ever use it. The kids don't either, because the only kids here at the eco-farm are me and Astrid's little boy, Tiger, and he's only a baby, so he can hardly get up there on his own. Not unless he climbed on the back of one of the goats and then—

"WANDA!" says Elif, trying to catch my attention.

"What?" I ask.

"Were you saying something to me?" repeats Elif. "When you were looking at the ground just now?"

Oops, I must've mumbled all the yoghurt-spoon words out loud without realising. But I perk up, glad Elif's awake. I thought she was dozing, like the goats. The herd must all be snoozing, by the pines and the pond – I can't hear their bells.

"That's Spanish and Swedish and Thai for 'Hi,

my name is Wanda!'," I tell her, pointing out my doodles in the dirt. "And I can introduce myself in a whole bunch of OTHER languages, like Dutch and Greek and Arabic and Hebrew and Italian. And cos we're in France right now, I should say, 'Bonjour, je m'appelle Wanda!'."

I don't mention it, but I can also say 'Hi' in Turkish ('Merhaba!') and German ('Tag!'). The reason I don't mention it is because Elif is Turkish-German so that'd hardly be big news to her.

"Uh-huh," Elif nods, lifting her sunglasses onto her head and staring down at me.

She doesn't say anything else, so I keep talking, cos I don't like silences.

"Do you know what 'posso comprar abacaxi' means?" I ask her, but then before Elif can reply I tell her. "It's 'Can I buy some pineapple' in Portuguese. And then when we were living in Ibiza, Patti was working in this café on the beach and I memorised ALL the flavours in Spanish on the ice-cream menu. My favourite flavour is 'chicle', cos it means 'bubblegum', but it sounds more like a TICKLE, doesn't it?"

Elif raises her dark eyebrows and 'huh's again.

I don't know if she's impressed or not, but it's okay – she never sounds bored when I talk, like some of the other backpackers and travellers me and my mum have met along the way. Lots of them sort of glaze over when I'm chatting or else laugh and say stuff like, "Wow, you *sure* can talk, kid!" which I don't think they mean in a particularly nice way.

"Hey, try this . . ." Elif says something I don't understand.

"What?" I mumble. I've sort of forgotten what we were just talking about because my hamster wheel of a brain is rattling away at top speed, like normal. MY normal.

Elif repeats the words I don't recognise, and then I guess that she's trying to teach me something in Turkish maybe. It doesn't sound like German.

I concentrate on the rhythm and shape of the words she just said and do my best to repeat them. Words in Turkish sound heavy and important. Same with German, actually.

"Annen . . . keçiye . . . benziyor . . ." I say slowly and carefully.

Elif bursts out laughing.

"Did I say it wrong?" I ask.

I worry a lot about getting things wrong. I want people to like me. I THINK Elif likes me. Same as both her native languages, she can seem very serious, till she smiles and then her whole face lights up. She's twenty-three and is travelling around in her beat-up campervan till her money runs out (or her campervan breaks down), same as everyone we get to know at the hostels and communes and farms we tend to stay at.

It's our story too; me and Patti's. Though Patti is thirty-four (and I'm twelve). And we travel on trains and buses and ferries. Our money hasn't run out for the last three years, but that's cos Patti picks up work wherever we go, and cos Patti got a bunch of money after Gran died and her bungalow got sold. Patti says that as long as we're careful with money, we can go on and on and on travelling as long as we like.

On and on and on . . .

It sounds a LOT sometimes.

"No, you said it perfectly!" says Elif, reaching a long, light brown leg out towards me and gently pushing me on the shoulder with her bare toes.

But I've forgotten what we were just talking about. Again.

"Huh?"

Elif was laughing at something I said . . .

"I taught you to say, 'My mother looks like a goat'!"

Wow! You know something? Elif is right. My mum DOES look like a goat. And I know the exact goat. It's Babette, of course, the really pretty goat on the farm who has shaggy white fur and amazingly pale eyes. Kenzo – a Japanese student who worked here till last week – took a photo of Patti and Babette posing together, with Patti's white-blonde dreads all piled on top of her head, and her ice-blue eyes twinkling at the camera. I swear Patti and Babette looked more like mum and daughter than me and Patti do. I mean, if someone saw me and Elif right now, I bet they'd think WE were related. We've both got matching tangles of dark hair and everything. She could be my big sister or cousin or something. (It must be nice to have a big sister or cousin or something.)

"Hey, don't take offence," Elif says casually. "I'm joking!"

Honestly, I hadn't been remotely offended that Elif had compared Patti to a goat. But then again, did she

MEAN to be mean? I don't think Elif likes my mum too much. Elif's smile slides off her face whenever Patti comes into the room, or passes in the distance, or says something, or laughs, or BREATHES, even.

I think it's cos of Jakub, the backpacker from Poland who's staying here too. He stares all lovey-dovey at my mum quite a lot of the time, and maybe Elif would like him to look at HER that way. I want to tell Elif that Patti doesn't feel lovey-dovey about Jakub. For a start, she's WAAAAYYYYY older than him. And Patti is always friendly to everyone, wherever we stay and wherever she works, whether that's on a farm helping pick crops like she's doing now, or teaching English for a term, or working in ice-cream shops at the seaside. All the time I've known Patti – which is basically for ever, obviously – she's never had a boyfriend (or girlfriend).

Though she DID have a boyfriend once upon a time, or I wouldn't be here, would I?

"Hey, Wanda . . . where did you go just now?" asks Elif, gently nudging me with her toe again. She's spotted that I just got lost in the babble inside my own head. Which makes a change from babbling out loud, I suppose.

"I'm here!" I say, waving up at her. "Honest!"

"So you heard what I just said?"

"Yeah, you said sorry for joking about Patti being a goat!"

"No – not *that*," Elif says with a roll of her eyes. "I said what do you think about sailing around Indonesia?"

"Who's sailing around the where now?" I ask, scrunching up my nose.

"Indonesia! Your mum and Jakub have been talking about it a lot in the evenings, when you've gone to bed. Jakub knows someone who works on tourist boats there and they're looking for more staff."

Huh? Patti's said nothing to me about Indonesia. OR working on a boat.

But wait a sec; she *has* been doing that thing of giving me extra hugs and kisses. When she does that, it means she's super-excited about something and is figuring out how to tell me. Basically, it's every time she's decided it's time to pack up and move on. When I was younger, that meant different flats. Since we left the UK, it's meant different countries.

Dumb old me; I should've spotted the signs!

"When is it supposed to be happening?" I grill Elif.

"Not sure," she says, shrugging her shoulders in

the cocoon of the hammock. "Jakub's going to some silent meditation retreat first, in the mountains south of here. Then he's selling his motorbike and flying to Bali sometime after that."

I've heard of Bali. It's a famous holiday island in Indonesia, and Indonesia is made up of *loads* of islands, I think.

I try to think of other things I might know about Indonesia.

But all I can think is it is a long, long, LONG way away, and after three years of travelling I feel really, really, REALLY tired all of a sudden.

Elif is staring at me with her piercing dark eyes, trying to figure out what I make of the news, I'm sure.

For a second, I don't say anything. But the inside of my head is bursting as I picture me and Patti packing up everything AGAIN, saying goodbye to everyone AGAIN, trying to settle somewhere new AGAIN.

I throw my wooden spoon to one side and use both hands to frantically rub away all my hellos in the dirt.

Cos what's the point in leaving my name anywhere when I never stay long enough to feel like I'm real?

MARGOT

Dear Diary,

I hate Charlie!

So today was the last day of term before the summer holidays, i.e. the most fun day of school in the whole year. The teachers absolutely don't care any more and for once we don't have to wear stupid school uniform.

I was planning on wearing my skinny jeans with the turn-ups. Dad ironed them last night and hung them over the back of the kitchen chair with a bunch of other ironing. But when I went to put my jeans on this morning, Charlie had spooned cornflakes into the turn-ups. Soggy, milky cornflakes!!

"Aw, that's so not cool, Charlie!" my dad said when

he heard me losing my mind.

"Oh, Charlie . . ." Mum sighed, walking into the kitchen with Charlie's bag for school. Charlie just looked around at us all and smiled so wide that milk dribbled down his chin. Honestly, that kid can be so disgusting.

But you know what makes me really lose my mind? How laid-back Dad is about all the stuff Charlie does. I mean, yes, he is only four. But it's like living with a wild mongoose sometimes. He totally tornadoes around the house destroying whatever's in front of him. I mean, just this week he drew all over my white trainers with his crayons 'to make them pretty' and made a potion in the back garden with mud, Dad's shaving foam and my new nail varnish.

And when that sort of stuff happens, Mum at least has a chat with him. Before bed last night I heard her telling Charlie that if he could please just remember where he put the house phone that would be really, really useful cos our Grandad Pops doesn't believe in mobiles and will only make contact via the landline. (Nice try, Mum, but Charlie can never remember where he puts anything.) Dad, on the other hand, just seems to think that everything Charlie does is insanely cute and adorable.

So I know this sounds bad, but after I got changed into my second favourite pair of jeans this morning, I had to turn away and hide my grin when Dad couldn't find his mobile.

"Did you take it, Charlie?" I heard him say to my brother in this sing-song voice that just makes Charlie giggle. "Is it in the same place you put the house phone? Do you want to show me where they both are?"

Of course Charlie didn't! Dad was turning this into an excellent game!

Anyway, I was moaning to Marisa about Charlie and Dad on the way to school but I could tell she wasn't really listening. And why would she, when she's flying to Sicily later this evening? I can't believe my best friend has the cheek to desert me for the whole summer. I hate her mum for taking her away that long to visit relatives. And I'm so jealous that Marisa has a really cool older sister to hang out with. I mean, Toni gives Marisa all the clothes and stuff she *doesn't want any more – how brilliant would that be? All I get from Charlie is slobbery kisses and the occasional bite on the arm.*

And think about it; next week, Marisa and Toni will be at the beach, while I'll be on a 'mini-break' in wellies on a farm in the drizzle. And while Marisa and her sister will be wandering around the shops and cafés in sunny Palermo, I'll be trailing after my little brother while he chucks food pellets at goats and sheep, cos Mum and Dad say ALL our holidays have to be little-kid-friendly, i.e. not remotely suitable for fourteen-year-old girls like me.

So, yeah, looks like the whole summer is going to be this endless, boring void. Great.

Night, night, Diary . . .

#Gloom

#BoredAlready

FRIDAY

WANDA

I'm scratching MADLY at my head as I walk towards the farm office. I think I might have nits again. (Thanks, Tiger.)

Having another nit-attack is bad news because Patti doesn't believe in 'toxic' chemicals, so she'll just tug at my hair for hours with a tiny comb, and after all that I'll just end up with a really sore head and STILL have nits.

There's lots of stuff that Patti doesn't believe in. Like labels; she hates them. Not labels on clothes, though – labels stuck on people. She thinks if you call people 'Mum' or 'Dad' then that's a kind of label and you take away their personality. That's why I call her Patti. And I have no one to call 'Dad' anyway. (I tried calling Gran 'Sharon' once when I was little and that did NOT go down well.) Oh, and Patti hated it when I was in school back at home and my teacher Mrs Chopra asked if Patti had ever considered the fact that I might have ADHD? After the meeting, Patti starting crying, saying that it's shocking and terrible to put labels on young kids and not just appreciate their individuality.

The thing is, I know Patti understands life a lot better than me. But I think I maybe understand ME better than she does. The truth I can't tell Patti is that I'd quite like to call her 'Mum'. It sounds like a warm hug. And Mrs Chopra saying that stuff about ADHD? It kind of make sense of the jumble I feel inside . . .

Anyway, I don't have time to think about labels or my old teacher (I loved her) or nits (hate them) right now.

I've got Komodo dragons on my mind. Komodo dragons and orangutans. Komodo dragons and orangutans and macaque monkeys. Cos I'm pretty sure Indonesia is where they're all from. And while it would be INSANELY cool to see a real, live Komodo dragon and an orangutan and a macaque, I need to check if you actually DO get them in Indonesia. That way I can be prepared, so that Patti doesn't try and bamboozalise me with all the amazing things we'll see if we go there. Basically, I don't want to be surprised and wowed by what she has to say; I want to be cross with her for making plans without me. Like always.

So before Patti finishes work this afternoon, I'll Google everything I can about sailing holidays around the islands of Indonesia. And to Google anything, I have to ask Hélène in the farm office building if I can use the spare computer. (Even if it's ancient and slow, at least it isn't a small very un-smart phone like the mobile Patti lets me have for emergencies. The phone that has absolutely nothing on it but Patti's number.)

"Hi, Hélène!" I say, blink-blinking into what feels like the gloom of the office after the blinding summer light outside in the yard. "Comment allez-vous?"

Patti always says adults are very impressed with young people who bother to ask how they are, so that's what I make sure I do, cos it's nice to make Patti proud of me. Though Patti is ALWAYS proud of me.

Whenever we move (which is often) and wherever we move to (which is lots of different places), she'll tell all the new people we meet how brilliant I am at languages and gets me to rattle off all the little bits and bobs I know.

But I'm not brilliant, not really. I'm useless in disguise. It's like if you picture a language as if it's a whole bunch of rain – like a storm or something – then all I'M ever able to say is about as tiny as a smeck of a raindrop. And yes, I know 'smeck' isn't even a proper word. Neither is 'bamboozalise'. See? I don't even know enough words in ENGLISH – which is the language I'm meant to know best – that I sometimes just make words up. Mum says that's a super cool talent but it's not. It's really, really not.

"Hi, Wanda!"

I jump when someone who isn't Hélène answers me. I get used to the low light and make out Astrid. Astrid is from Denmark, which is famous for Lego and having lots of islands (four hundred and forty-four – I looked it up) and for not having a word in their language for 'please'. Patti and me share the loft room above the barn with her, and her baby

Tiger. All the rest of the farm workers are housed in mobile homes in the field next to the main buildings. Elif came late in the season so that there was no space left in any of those, and she was offered the single bed that's also in our big loft room. Funnily enough, when she walked up the rickety outside steps to the loft and heard Tiger yelling himself awake from his afternoon nap, Elif straightaway clattered right back down the wooden stairs. Now the single bed is just where she dumps her rucksack and clothes and stuff, while she sleeps peacefully in her campervan.

I spot that Astrid is standing by the humming office printer. Tiger is sitting at her feet, playing with one of her flip-flops, flip-flapping it noisily on the floor.

"Hi, Astrid," I say back. "Hello, puttemus!!"

That last word is aimed at Tiger. It means 'little mouse who likes to cuddle' in Danish, which sounds very sweet, and Tiger mostly is sweet, except at night when he wakes up and does his scream-crying, which is zero fun.

"Are you okay, Wanda?" asks Astrid, tilting her head to one side. She looks like a toy herself, like some doll with her hair in two braids and her round apple cheeks.

For a second I wonder what she means, till I realise I must've been frowning. Quickly, I slap on my usual smile and step over Tiger towards the computer.

Now I can see that Hélène is on the phone at her desk. She gives me the thumbs-up, assuming I'm here to do some random chunk of schoolwork, which I try to do a bit of every day. (Though I get sidetracked a lot and start off doing stuff like a test on equations and then end up Googling how many islands Denmark has.)

"Just wondering about something, going to look it up," I tell Astrid. "Oh, are you still using the computer?"

Something official-looking is on the screen.

"I'll be done in a minute," says Astrid. "We're flying home to Copenhagen next Sunday, but I need a copy of a permission letter for Tiger."

Part of me wonders who'll do all the catering if Astrid's leaving, since that's her job here. But then it seems like me and Patti might not be around for long either, if Elif's right.

"What do you mean, 'permission letter'?" I ask her.

"Me and Tiger have different names on our passports; he has his dad's surname," explains Astrid. "So I need to have a copy of Tiger's birth certificate and a copy of this letter from my ex, saying I have his permission to travel alone with Tiger. Just in case anyone questions us at Customs in different countries."

My surname's Bain, same as Patti, so we don't have that problem. Patti and Wanda Bain.

I wonder what my dad's surname even was?

Patti says she can't remember. She says he was just a sweet boy called Lee, who she met and loved forever ago, in another life and time, in a whirlwind golden summer of travelling around the Greek islands . . .

She makes it sound so romantic. I wish it was less romantic and more *real*. I wish I had a photo of Lee to see if my freckles are HIS freckles. If his ears stick out like mine do. If he has a little gap between his teeth, same as me.

And then I tune into Astrid again and realise she's still talking. "Tiger smeared his porridge on our old permission letter so I'm printing out a new one . . ."

Astrid looks down fondly at Tiger, who's now clanging the flip-flop off a metal chair leg and squealing at his new game.

Over at her desk, Hélène frowns at the racket. I don't think she totally approves of Patti or Astrid, travelling around with kids. The day me and Patti turned up at the eco-farm she looked shocked at the sight of me tagging along. I suppose Patti just forgot to mention my existence, when she got in touch about the live-in summer job here.

It's very complicated when people – like Elif and Hélène – like ME, but don't particularly like my mum, if you see what I mean. I wish I could get them to understand that Patti loves me and just wants to give me the best, most interesting life. Even if I don't want it.

"Wanda! Babycakes!" says Patti, suddenly appearing in the office doorway with a big smile and a slightly worried expression. She waves at me to follow her outside. So much for my Googling session.

I follow her out, with a quick "ouch!" as Tiger whacks my ankle with a rubbery slap of a flip-flop.

"Come here, Sweetpea!" Patti carries on, leading

me to the one of the well-worn plastic sets of patio tables and chairs that are dotted around the yard. A tilted and torn parasol flutters above the table that Patti opts for.

I sit.

Like the extra hugs and kisses, she's overdoing the 'Babycakes' and 'Sweetpeas'.

Here it comes.

"So, Elif says she mentioned the Indonesia plan to you?" Patti begins, leaning her elbows on the wobbly table and looking earnestly at me. "She says she didn't realise that I hadn't spoken to you about it . . ."

I notice that my mum – with her tangled crown of dreads – has her head tilted in a way that exactly matches the angle of the wonky parasol that's shading us.

Patti starts talking.

She's saying stuff.

Stuff about the job on the tourist boat that she might take.

Stuff about an amazing opportunity to see so much of Indonesia.

Stuff about the awesome landscapes we'd see.

Stuff about the incredible nature we'd witness and hey, don't I love nature?

Stuff about Komodo dragons and orangutans and macaque monkeys (I knew it!).

Stuff about how lucky I am compared to any normal kid my age.

And for a while I don't say anything; I just stare at the wonky parasol and at my mum, feeling like I'm stuck behind glass, shouting but not being heard.

But then I vaguely do make out Patti saying something.

"Wanda! Babycakes! Sweetpea!" she's calling out, and I realise I'm sobbing and sobbing and sobbing.

And now I'm in her arms and snuffling wetly into her shoulder about what's the POINT of awesome landscapes and incredible nature and Komodo dragons and orangutans and macaque monkeys if I'm stuck on my own in a cabin on a ship or a yacht or whatever kind of boat thing it is while she works for stupid tourists or whoever and anyway how can she say how lucky I am compared to any normal kid my age when I DON'T KNOW any other kids my age?

Patti is rocking me, which is wonderful and I love it. And she is mumbling something that makes me take a deep breath, that gives me hope for a second. That makes the rollercoaster stop for a minute.

"Okay, my darling, my sweet Wanda, I hear you," mutters Patti, my lovely, loving mum, cuddling me tight. "And hey, hold on; I've just thought of something else . . ."

I listen to what Patti has to say, with my heart pounding and full of hope.

But it's a terrible idea.

TERRIBLE.

MARGOT

Dear Diary,

That stuff I wrote last night . . . I don't really hate Charlie. I love the disgusting little mongoose.

And I don't really hate Marisa's mum. She makes really great Italian food and asks me to stay for dinner all the time. (Though there've not been so many of those 'just-stay-for-dinner' moments lately. Since Nana died we've had to have lots of compulsory-attendance family meals at home with Grandad Pops.)

Also, about the petting farm place we're going to in a couple of days . . . The truth is, I'm quite looking forward to chucking food pellets at goats and sheep, though I'm definitely not admitting that to Mum and Dad.

What I'm not looking forward to is the fact that Grandad Pops is coming along with us. I know that sounds mean, but since Nana died last year he's become like a happiness vacuum. I mean, we all miss her madly – cos she was totally the best, kindest, most fun nan ever – but we're not grumpy and mean in our sadness like he sometimes is.

Saying that, I'm a bit grumpy myself today. I never check out boring Facebook too much, but I'm on Mum's page or whatever it's called and she's posted this photo of her and Dad with Charlie at his school sports day last week. It's not the photo that's got me grumpy (it's pretty cute of the three of them laughing together cos Charlie's stuck his prize of a red rosette on his forehead); it's the comments that really hacked me off. The first one was from one of Mum's friends who wrote "Ooh, perfect little family!". After that there were tons of comments practically the same; Mum, Dad and Charlie. Perfect, perfect, perfect. The rule of three.

Only there's four of us.

Though Charlie is so full on and sucks up just about all of Mum and Dad's energy, so it's no wonder

no one notices me, Diary. I feel like I take up about 10%
of the space and attention in this family.

And have I gone completely invisible to Marisa?
I sent her a bunch of these really funny memes of
goats headbutting people (i.e. what's probably going
to happen to ME next week) and she hasn't got back
to any of them . . .

#HelloCanAnyoneSeeMe
#HelloHelloHello

SATURDAY

WANDA

It's time to say goodbye to my mum.

The terrible idea she thought of yesterday is to take off on her own for a few days. Well, not on her *own* exactly; she's tagging along with Jakub to the meditation retreat he'd booked into.

A few days in the peace of the mountains will sort her head out, she said.

Figure out the next long-term steps for me and her, she said.

"You understand, don't you, Sweetpea?" Patti asks, pushing my hair back from my face.

We're sitting at the top of the open wooden staircase that leads to the loft room. The peach of the dawn is rising above the trees on the hillside and the breeze is chilly round my bare legs. (I'm wearing Patti's favourite band T-shirt that she's kept from the '90s – can you believe something could be that old? I'm using it as a nightie cause both my PJs are for 'age 10', and they don't fit me any more. Patti keeps saying we'll go shopping for new ones but we haven't had the time yet. Like two years of no time.)

"Mmm," I mutter, moving away from my mum's hug, because I'm worried that I'll get a splinter in my bum sitting where I am. Or that I'll start crying.

"And you'll be fine with Astrid taking care of you while I'm away, right?"

"Uh-huh," I agree, hearing Astrid snoring in the double bed inside the room behind us, picturing Tiger spread out like a pudgy pale pink starfish beside her.

"I know it's going to be weird us not speaking for a whole week, Wanda," says Patti, staring at me even more earnestly, which makes me look at the dawn even harder. "But the retreat is really strict about locking phones and computers away for the whole time you're there. Just so we have no distractions from finding our inner answers."

No distractions . . .

I'M the distraction, aren't I? I'M making Patti unhappy and stopping her doing what she wants to do. She'd be better off taking her 'next long-term steps' without stupid, annoying little ME holding her back . . .

"But look, you've got the emergency number, haven't you?" Patti checks, nodding at the phone in my hand. Of course I have the emergency number for the office at the retreat. She's just inputted it in my not-a-smartphone herself. If something major happens I can call it. "But there won't be an emergency, Wanda, I promise."

How can Patti promise that? Anything could happen. I could get appendicitis or whooping cough or impetigo or scarlet fever or shingles or about a million other illnesses that I read about in a thick-as-a-brick book called *Your Health Manual* that I found in the 'English' section of a charity shop in Portugal last year. I read it in about a week – all of it – while Patti was teaching English. I remember Patti laughing at the time because she spotted that it was published forever ago in 1972. But at least I'll know the symptoms of ringworm if she suddenly comes down with it.

And it's got nothing to do with worms, weirdly.

Patti tries again to hug me, but I stand up immediately and say bye to her in as many languages as I can remember – as fast as I can – because it helps stop me from crying.

"I'd better go, darling . . . Jakub's waving at me to hurry up."

And with that – plus a bunch of blown kisses – Patti tippetty-taps down the stairs to Jakub and the motorbike idling below, waiting to take her away from me.

It's so early still that I try going back to bed after that, but can't sleep.

I pretend to, even with the whispered racket Astrid and Tiger make when they get up and dressed. I still keep pretending, even when Tiger comes over and tries to wake me by blowing raspberries in my face.

But once I hear the noise and clatter of Astrid and her helpers getting breakfast ready in the barn building below me – and then the muffled chatter of the farm workers arriving to eat – I decide to sneak out to somewhere I feel comfy and safe . . .

Only now that I'm lying in the small, dusty space

in the dark, I don't feel comfy and safe at all. My head is maddeningly itchy (stupid nits) and all I can think about is possible emergencies that I hadn't even thought about till now. I mean . . .

- What if Jakub is a terrible driver?
- What if his puttering old motorbike is veering catastrophically off the motorway at this exact second?
- What if Patti is lying in a ditch, in terrible pain and weeping cos I wouldn't let her hug me when she was leaving?
- What if it's ALL MY FAULT?
- What if I've made something really BAD happen to my mum because I was angry with her, and the last thing she'll remember before she passes away is me practically yelling, "AU REVOIR!! ADIOS!! AUF WIEDERSEHEN!!" at her?
- What if—

"Wanda?" Elif interrupts my panicked thoughts. "You want to come out from under there?"

She holds up the cloth that covers the empty storage space below the long seat in the back of her campervan. I wriggle out.

"What are you doing in here?" she asks – but doesn't sound annoyed. She sits down on the matching long seat opposite, her crumpled pillow and rumpled sleeping bag on it from last night.

"I sometimes come here to get away, when it gets too noisy," I tell her, as I wriggle out and kneel on the lino floor, brushing bobbles of dust away from my T-shirt nightie. "The lock on the back door of the van is broken . . ."

I sneak in here quite a lot, specially in the evenings. The barn is like a living room for all the helpers who work on the farm, so after dinner they hang out in there and chat and laugh and get louder and louder and *louder* as the evening wears on.

"Yeah, I keep meaning to get the lock fixed," Elif says with a nod. "So, hey – I heard your mother actually did it? She left you?"

I feel a sudden flash of anger towards Elif. Yes, maybe I AM furious with Patti, but no one else is allowed to make out that she's being a rubbish mum. Even if she is.

"It's just for a week. She'll be back on Saturday!" I say defensively. "And it's not like she's left me alone . . . Astrid's looking after me."

Elif mutters something under her breath that I'm pretty sure is a German swear word.

"Wanda, I wouldn't leave Astrid in charge of the goats, never mind my own daughter!" she says, in that sort-of-funny, sort-of-never-been-more-serious way of hers.

And then all my irritation melts away like a snowball chucked in a bath.

Astrid IS a bit useless.

"Remember that morning when she was meditating in your room, and she didn't notice that Tiger had crawled outside, bumped down an entire flight of stairs on his bottom and got himself in the henhouse?"

I did. Tiger stole all the eggs meant for breakfast and chucked them at the goats.

"And wasn't there a time before I arrived," Elif carries on, "when Astrid was meditating in front of a candle and leant over it and set fire to one of her braids?"

"Yeah . . . I remember that," I say with a nod. "Burnt hair smells of VILE-ness."

Elif frowns at my sort of made-up word.

"I mean it stank out our room for DAYS," I explain. "Patti had to ask her nicely not to light candles in the loft ever again because they're not exactly safe."

Elif is in the middle of a humongous eye-roll when we hear an uncomfortably loud, unsettlingly high-pitched sound. The fire alarm!

In a split-second, I'm out of the van, running towards the barn, cos the alarm is coming from that direction. What's also coming from that direction is smoke spiralling out of the open windows and doorway.

As I run, I spot Hélène, standing frozen by the office building. And I can see some of the workers in the distance, running back from the fields. But I can beat them to it.

"Les pompiers! Les pompiers! 112 – vite!" I call out to Hélène, who shakes herself out of her shock-freeze, grabs her mobile from her pocket and dials fast.

I've read a lot about ADHD (i.e. the condition my mum doesn't want to admit I have) and I know that my brain is like a runaway train, which can be – IS – completely exhausting most of the time. But here are two things that are ACE about my runaway trainwreck of a brain . . .

1) I am VERY good in a crisis and don't panic at all (though I am *excellent* at panicking in normal life).

2) I am AWESOME when it comes to learning stuff I'm interested in (though pretty terrible with stuff that bores me). And so I've learnt the names of every emergency service in each country me and Patti have stayed in. 'Pompiers' is French for 'firefighters'. In all of the European Union countries you dial 112 for help. In Thailand you call 191. In Morocco it's 12/112 for police, 15 for fire brigade and 150 for ambulance. In Egypt they have a 'tourist' police number (126) but Patti said that wouldn't refer to us if we were in need of help, because we were travellers and

not silly tourists. I wonder what the emergency numbers are in Indonesia, if me and Patti do end up go—

"What do we do?" yells Elif, catching up with me.

"Make sure they're all right!" I tell her, as I see Astrid run out of the building with Tiger kicking and screaming in her arms.

"Is anyone else in there?" I yell at Astrid, and am immediately relieved to see her shake her head. That's good, but there's still a fire to deal with. If it burns down the barn, it'll burn down the loft room above it, including all our stuff! Me and Patti may travel light, but I'm NOT about to lose my framed photo of Gran or my passport or my beloved and battered teddy Theo in his little blue waistcoat.

And so I grab the hose in the yard, turn on the tap and blast a fierce stream of water through the open window of the barn. (Rule number one: never go into a burning building. But technically, I'm still outside.)

I aim the powerful arc of water through the smoke towards the narrow tower of flames I can now see in the middle of the room, where beanbags slump on the ratty old rug. The smell is *awful*; worse than the burnt hair stench in our room that time Astrid's braid caught alight.

With angry hissing, the fire and flames quickly surrender to the soaking, and I can make out a blackened beanbag that looks like it's melted into the rug.

Then all of a sudden the noise of people smothers me. Voices and bodies and arms are reaching in. A strong pair of hands insistently lifts the surprisingly heavy hose from mine, which are shaking madly.

And from the long, snaking road up to the farm comes the blare of sirens, which means the 'pompiers' are on their way from the nearby village.

"Well done, Wanda!" I hear someone say, patting my shoulder.

More hearty thumps on my shoulders.

More talk of the relief that there's no damage except the blackened rug and half-a-beanbag. There's just the horrible, cloying smoke to deal with.

But of course that's going to be drifting up into our room right now, wrapping itself around mine and Patti's things, making them stink, ruining them!

Leaving the babble of voices behind me, I shoot off to the side of the building, where I leap up the wooden steps to the loft, two at a time.

Pushing the door open, I see drifts of dying smoke sneaking up through the floorboards.

Okay, I can't carry EVERYTHING out, so I'll just stuff my few precious things into my rainbow-patterned canvas bag. Other stuff like spare clothes can be washed and dried in the sunshine later.

With my things sorted, I'm halfway over to Astrid's bed – about to grab the soft-toy tiger that baby-human Tiger likes to sleep with – when my eyes land on Patti's rucksack. Is there anything in there that my mum wouldn't want tainted with the smell of scorched and toxic polystyrene beanbag beads? I know Patti will have her passport and documentation with her at the retreat, just in case, but all the same I hurry over and quickly rifle through the rucksack's main sections and many pockets.

It's mostly just shorts and vest tops, a couple of hoodies and less favourite jewellery in there, plus a couple of dog-eared language phrase books.

But still, I come across a folder of Patti's paper qualifications and stuff; THAT'S got to be important. Then in a zipped pocket on the inside of the rucksack, my hand slides around a smaller plastic folder. Like, envelope-sized and clear.

Pulling it out, I smile as I see it holds a bunch of photos – the one on the top is of Patti and a tiny version of me on holiday. My hair is short with tight dark curls (wonder if I had nits then?). Patti's is blonde as ever but long and straight. We were on holiday in Ireland somewhere, wherever Gran was from. Gran took the photo, which is a bit blurry (her speciality).

I'm shaking all the photos out of the plastic folder and onto the floorboards to get a better look at them when Elif comes in, hurrying over to the single bed.

"Ach, it smells horrible in here!" she announces.

I don't answer because she's right, it IS horrible. And also, I'm too caught up in these images that are spread out in front of me. I'm just surprised to find that Patti kept some family photos with her while we've been travelling. I had no idea. I thought any actual photos like these were in the couple of albums and frames packed up in boxes in the rented storage unit back home in the UK.

"You know why the fire started, Wanda? It was Astrid and one of her stupid candles again! She was going to meditate in the barn after breakfast but dropped the lit candle when she tripped over a toy of Tiger's," Elif explains angrily, as she starts shoving all her jeans and tops and trainers into her rucksack and holdalls. "She's down in the yard right now crying and saying she'll leave straight away if Hélène wants her to. Can you believe this?"

What I can't believe is how lovely it is to see all these photos with Gran in them! I suddenly miss her x 100. Patti always says Gran was a bit bossy, but I don't remember her like that. Even when I was little I kind of thought Gran was just worried about Patti and about me and how much we moved from rented flat to rented flat. I think Gran would've liked it if we'd gone to live with her. She loved both of us so much.

Look at this photo now: of Gran sharing a cloud of candyfloss with the tiny me at a fair. And this squished-together selfie of me and Patti and Gran at a Christmas market in town, with a giant lit-up reindeer behind us – its antlers look like they're growing out of Gran's head! And what's this one?

Oh . . .

This photo isn't Christmassy; it's very, very summery. The background is of blue skies, turquoise sea and white buildings. Like Crete, where me and Patti went last spring.

But my heart starts thundering as I realise it's NOT a photo of the two of us, of my mum Patti and me. It's of a young couple . . . a guy, a girl, in their early twenties, maybe? The pale girl has dark sunglasses on, a smile so wide, and with cute, white-blonde space-buns. The boy has his arm around her shoulders. He has soft brown skin, head shaved close, a smile that shows off his front teeth with a cute gap. He's wearing board shorts and a pale grey T-shirt with a band name on it.

I look down at my lookalike nightie. My mum's precious relic from the '90s. It says 'Nirvana' on it, same as the T-shirt the young man in the photo is wearing.

Whoah . . .

There's still another couple of photos to see.

With my fingers trembling, I lift up the next one . . .

The young woman – my mum – is clutching something to her, a teddy, in a blue waistcoat. The pocket of the bear's waistcoat is a tiny Greek flag, blue and white. The person taking the photo is not in shot, but they have one hand reached out to the younger Patti, and she is holding that hand to her cheek. She has no sunglasses on now, and her eyes are full, full, FULL of love.

Immediately, I reach into my rainbow bag and pull out Teddy Theo. He is worn and scruffy, but his blue waistcoat is still intact. I hadn't even thought that the faded pattern on the pocket of its waistcoat was supposed to be the Greek flag.

"This place is crazy!" I vaguely hear Elif moan. "I was going to leave at the end of the season and visit my cousins in London. But after this, I think I'll go tomorrow. As soon as I get my wages from Hélène . . ."

I feel like my whole body is shifting, changing.

I'm not in it any more.

I'm watching from the ceiling of the loft as I spread all the photos out, as Elif moves and talks on the other side of the room.

I'm staring down over the shoulder of me (Wanda), and I can see that the last photo is just a headshot of the young man. He's grinning his warm, gap-toothed grin. Behind him is blue water, a harbour full of bobbing boats with (more) blue-and-white Greek flags. He has a smattering of dark freckles across his light brown skin. His ears stick out just a little, like mine.

My heart starts to judder.

"You need to call your mother straight away; tell her to turn around and come back from her silly trip," I hear Elif say, as I watch from my strange angle up on the ceiling.

But I don't want to think about my mother right now, or I will just be so incredibly ANGRY I might COMBUST, like the fire that just happened down in the barn. Why has Patti kept these photos with her, like they're precious? And why hasn't she ever shared them with ME?

"Wanda?" I hear Elif say. "Are you listening to me? What is wrong?"

I'm too stunned to answer because the me down

below has just flipped the last photo over and read the message scribbled on the back of it.

'Love you, Patti.

Look me up when you get back to the UK.

Lee xxx'

And then there's an address scrawled underneath the message. An address in a place called Dover.

Wait a sec; I've heard of Dover! It's a place where you can get the ferry to France. Actually, I think it goes to and from Calais, which is just a couple of hours away from here. Me and my mum didn't travel that route when we left the UK three years ago; we went from Portsmouth to Bilbao in Spain, cos Patti had an old friend there who had a spare room and knew of a restaurant job Patti could do and—

Hold on! Why does my brain always run off in different directions? Like a handful of chucked marbles? Ferries and where they go or don't go doesn't matter right now, does it? What matters is this address. An address where Lee does – or used to – live.

Lee.

Lee Lee Lee.

LEEEEEEEEEEEEEE!!!

My DAD!

OMG my, actual DAD . . .

"Wanda? Wanda – talk to me!"

Elif's voice drifts up to me in the ceiling.

I look down at Elif and the me that's below.

"It's all right," I say, as I slide back down and fit neatly back inside myself. "It's all going to be okay."

And it is.

Because Patti has always taken me along on all her adventures.

But maybe now it's time I had one all of my own . . ..

MARGOT

Hi Diary,

So Grandad Pops came round tonight for dinner, and to talk about our mini-break to the farm. It was all fine, all normal, till he went and said something properly bad.

While everyone was trying to eat their carbonara and have a chat, Charlie was running round naked, with some of Mum's lipstick smeared on his face, and making a noise that was supposed to be the roar of a shark, even though I always tell him sharks can't roar. Pops looked at Charlie with this glower – like a mix of confusion and disappointment – then turned to Dad and said, "Me and your mother would never have put up with that behaviour when *you were little, Louis!"*

Can you believe it?!?

Mum definitely couldn't. She went a bit stiff and shocked and silent, while Dad tried to grab Charlie for a sort of cuddle/restraint. Which made Charlie wriggle and shriek all the more.

And then came Pops' next really bad comment.

"I mean, I don't expect my only grandchild to be a saint," Pops grumbled. "But you and Gill have got to reign Charlie in, Louis."

His 'only' grandchild.

I mean, am I not Grandad Pops' grandchild too? Louis has been my dad since I was five years old, since him and Mum got together. I can't remember a time when he wasn't there, when he wasn't my game-playing, meal-cooking, school-picking-up real dad. More, much more than 'just' a stepdad.

And it was me who gave Grandad the nickname Pops in the first place!! When I first met him and Nana they introduced themselves as Nana Wanda and Grandad Paul. But I was only little and got muddled, and called him Pops instead of Paul, and it stuck, cos everyone thought it was so cute. (Well, maybe not

Grandad Pops himself. He doesn't really do 'cute'.)

But whatever, once Pops said the truly clunky thing about Charlie being his 'only' grandchild . . . I don't know whether it was me or Mum who stood up and left the table first, but all I could hear as I ran up the stairs to my room was Pops muttering, "What? What did I say? Oh, for goodness' sake, everyone is so touchy . . ."

Mum came to my room after a while to check if I was okay. I just said yes, cos I could see she'd been crying and didn't want to make her feel bad for me too.

I just wish I had someone I could talk to about this. I did try messaging Marisa but she's obviously having way too much fun with her sister Toni and all their Sicilian cousins to get back to me.

So it's just you and me, Diary! Just wish I had something fun to tell you instead of moaning all the time . . .

#FakeGranddaughter
#ThanksVeryMuchPops

SUNDAY

WANDA

Inside my annoying (and currently itchy) head, I sometimes have a ton of overlapping conversations going on with myself. Right now, on this journey, the yabbering feels so frantic and deafening that it's a wonder Elif can't hear it.

- This is the BEST idea I've ever had!
- No – it's the WORST idea I've ever had!!
- I think I'm going to sneeze—
- Don't sneeze!
- But it's so dusty under here!
- Oh, it's okay, the tickle in my nose has gone. (The itchiness on my head hasn't.)
- Aargh – what if someone's looking for me?

- Who'd be looking for me? Not Patti, that's for sure.
- THE POLICE! THE POLICE COULD BE LOOKING FOR ME!
- THE GENDARMES, I mean, since I'm still technically in France.
- That won't happen, though, cos I made sure no one would know where I went.
- Though maybe Hélène and Astrid didn't believe what I told them?
- My plan was SO good, though!
- The first part anyway.
- There're still more parts to it.
- Which means there's still time to muck everything up!
- No; stop panicking. EVERYTHING will be okay. MORE than okay – it'll be brilliant!
- ARRGHH! I've got cramp in my leg! Ouch!! OW!
- Of course you do – you've been hidden in this space since 6.30am. What did you expect?
- But who cares about cramp. I'm on my

way and NOTHING can stop me.

- Unless I get found out.
- Unless Elif finds out I'm stowing away in her van and goes mad at me.
- But once I'm on the ferry there's nothing she can do.
- Or can she? Will she tell someone official and they'll send me back?
- How would I even get back to the farm?
- Listen, I'm NOT going to get caught and I'm NOT going back there.
- I'm going to the UK. I'm on my way to Dover.
- Which is the best thing ever!
- Except I'm going to get into SO much trouble.
- SO, SO, SO much trouble.
- But it's absolutely WORTH IT!!!
- Uh-oh; the sneeze feels like it's coming back—
- Nope, gone again. Phew.
- I feel SICK I'm so excited.
- Or maybe I feel sick because I'm scared?
- If only I could magic the next few hours

away and just be there.

- I could try to sleep through the whole journey, I suppose. It'll probably be another couple of hours till we get to Calais and queue to get on the ferry. And then it's only about an hour or so till we cross the Channel and get to the UK.
- Go to sleep Wanda. SLEEP.
- SLEEEEEP!!!!!
- No chance; there's WAY too much adrenaline swooshing about inside of me to sleep.
- I mean, how can I sleep when I know I might MEET MY DAD SOON?!?
- And when I meet him, we'll talk and talk and talk and . . .
- *Zzzzz . . .*

Somewhere between the farm and the ferry I nodded off. Maybe it was cos of the rumbling of the campervan's engine shaking me like a baby in a buggy (or like Tiger when he'd ride around the fields on the tractor in Astrid's lap).

Or maybe it was cos of the dark; the morning light was blocked out with the thick cloth that hangs below the long seat here in the back (luckily, Elif had just shoved some walking boots and a parka into the storage space, so there was plenty of room for me to secretly wriggle in this morning when no one was looking).

Or maybe it was Elif's low voice as she sang and hummed along to some French radio station (bet she wouldn't be so chilled if she knew she wasn't travelling alone!).

But most probably it was because I slept for about two seconds last night on the fold-out bed in the farm office (the temporary accommodation Hélène sorted me out with while the loft room still stank of smoke).

Whatever it was, the time zapped past and I woke a few minutes ago to hear the metal clank and echo here in the depths of the ferry. I'm in the hold, in the car deck. I can hear doors upon doors slamming – including the driver's door of the campervan as Elif left just now – and then the blah-blah-blah of adults and shrieks of over-excited kids as they pass by on the way to the main decks upstairs.

So yeah, my plan had been to lie low, keeping myself safely stowed away in the hidey-hole in Elif's van till she'd driven off the ferry at the other end; the British end. But then I really, REALLY want to see the famous White Cliffs of Dover as we get close to the UK! (I looked up facts about Dover on the computer in the office last night.) And now I think about it, there's something else I really, REALLY wanted to do . . .

Here's the thing; I don't get to see TV too often and me and Patti never go to the movies. But what I do remember about films and series on the telly is that no one ever needs to go to the loo. Same goes for books. Characters can be having these amazing adventures through time and space, or going on epic quests or whatever, but no one ever needs to stop for a wee.

Well, it turns out *I* do, which is why I've wriggled out from under the seat and let myself out of the broken-locked van door, joining the crowds shuffling towards the lifts and stairwells. Above us there'll be cafes and restaurants and bars and video games to play and entertainers to watch. And toilets.

All I can think about is the crush of people, my full bladder and keeping my eyes out for Elif. But no matter how desperate I am, I'm smart, and so instead of queueing for the nearest toilets – where Elif might be! – I bolt to the far end of the ferry and find some empty loos there.

Ooh, the relief.

But now I've got a new urge; to EAT. I haven't had anything since yesterday teatime, when food was laid out on the patio tables for everyone to help themselves, since the smelly, smoky barn was out of action. And this morning, while Elif was helping herself to the bread and cheese laid out for breakfast, I was helping myself to a free ride home, by sneaking into her campervan.

Oh, I'm trying SO hard to ignore how good the burgers and chips smell as I pass fast-food outlets and happy families stuffing their faces! But I have to be careful with money. I mean, I've got some. Some Euros I found in Patti's rucksack yesterday, and a card for a bank account in the UK that Gran opened for me years ago.

But even with my gurgling empty tummy, it's fine, I think to myself, as I go out onto the open deck and breathe in the salty fresh air. Leaning my elbows on the rail, I stare down at the churn of the waves – and feel a sudden matching churn in my tummy.

Oh, I forgot I ALWAYS get seasick. That ferry from Portsmouth to Bilbao . . . the trip to Krk island in Croatia . . . the boat ride between Ibiza and Formentera . . . that sailing ship to the Blue Caves in Zakynthos . . . I have barfed in many, many scenic places and completely missed many, many spectacular views.

Actually, how come Patti forgot all that, when she was getting caught up in Jakub's plan to crew boats in Indonesia?

I'm about to be FURIOUS with her thoughtlessness all over again when my tummy gurgles ominously. Oh, please don't let me be si—

A hand clutches my upper arm, fingers pinching. White stars of panic pop in my eyes.

THE POLICE!

THE GENDARMES!!

"Don't arrest me!" I whimper, my eyes closed tight.

Then I hear a swear word in German and risk opening one eye.

It's Elif.

"Wanda! What are you *doing* here!!" she practically yells at me.

I take a deep breath, but everything stalls.

I'm numb, stuck, frozen.

All my ace plans seem WAY too complicated to explain.

"Wanda!" Elif repeats my name.

I'm the opposite of my chatterbox self.

My brain is full of thick fog, and my voice has disappeared.

It's all too much; this plan and all its risky parts.

It's like my hearing's gone on strike and everything's *sloooowwweeedd riiigghhht doownnnnn* . . .

I can see Elif's frown and her mouth moving, but I can't make out what she's saying. And then she's pulling me by the hand along the open deck, through doors, down stairs, and we're finally in the car deck and safely in her campervan.

I sit where she puts me, in the passenger seat next to her.

Back in this familiar environment, my senses start to unfurl.

"Wanda – I don't understand," I make out Elif

saying. "Are you ready to explain to me what's going on? Did you hide in my van all this way?"

Elif is my friend. Or as close as I have to a friend. I can tell her.

"Elif, I need to get to my dad, cos he's in Dover!" I blurt out. "I have his address. You can drop me there straight after we get off the ferry, and then you can go to your cousins in London and I'll be with my dad so everything will be okay!"

"Wait!" says Elif, holding up both hands. "Wanda, I remember you once told me that you didn't know your father."

Well, technically, I didn't till yesterday; till the fire in the barn and smoke in the loft and the secret packet of photos in Patti's rucksack. But I can't say any of this out loud or Elif will probably go FREAKTASTIC and refuse to take me to the address on the back of the photo.

I need a cover story, and quick.

"That's just what Patti made me say to people!" I lie. "Dad loves me and I love him. It's just that my mum's never wanted us to be together."

Elif frowns, confused.

I need to unconfusicate her QUICK.

"Patti doesn't care about me, Elif. My dad does. She's kept me from him for the last three years, always moving us around so he can't find us."

My tummy flips a bit. I don't like lying – it makes me feel ill. But I don't have another option right now. And I've been lying to more people than just Elif, since I came up with my plan to see Lee.

Elif growls a bit. I hear her mention Patti in that growl. My fibbing has clearly confirmed to her how useless Patti is as a parent.

"But wait," Elif says now, with a deep frown. "What about Astrid? Isn't she supposed to be looking after you?"

And now for my other lies.

"Didn't you notice Astrid and Tiger were gone this morning? They left for the airport before dawn. She wanted to go home to Denmark after the fire," I point out to her (this part is true). "I told Astrid that I'd be all right, that I'd contacted Patti and she was coming back from the retreat to get me today."

That second part was a lie, obviously. But I could see how relieved Astrid was when I said it to her last night. It meant she was free of the responsibility of me. She was free to leave.

"So Patti wasn't *really* coming for you?" asks Elif, her eyes like big brown moons of shock.

"No! I didn't call her. I just knew Patti would try and stop me from seeing my dad. She's jealous of how close we are!"

Oops, I should win an acting award, my lies are so good.

"But what about Hélène?" asks Elif. "She'll panic if you're gone. She was already angry with your mum for taking time off to go to the retreat and for leaving you behind."

"I told Hélène the same story, once I found out she was driving Astrid and Tiger to the airport," I explain. "I said that Patti was going to collect me and take me back to the retreat with her, and we'd both be back on Saturday."

The wonderful thing about yesterday's fire was that everything was sideways and back-to-front at the farm. Everyone was so preoccupied with the muddle of it all that they didn't do checks like they might have done any other time.

The chaos was PERFECT for a getaway.

"Okay, so you fooled Astrid and Hélène into thinking your mother was coming for you," says Elif. "But what happens next week, when your mum does come back from the mountains and sees that you're missing? What then?"

"It's okay – I've left her a letter explaining everything," I say, telling the truth here and picturing the envelope I taped to the top of Patti's rucksack in the loft room last night. "By then I'll have had some time with my dad. Patti can come get me after that, if she wants to. Her and Dad can work it out together."

I can see that sympathy is softening Elif's frown. A daughter and a dad cruelly separated by a mum who's stopping them from seeing each other . . . it's a heart-warming – though completely untrue – story. Elif's totally on my side.

Uh-oh, only she's suddenly frowning all over again, even HARDER this time!

"Wanda," Elif bursts out, "do you realise the trouble I'll be in if they find you hiding in my van? They will think I'm a people-smuggler!"

And now I feel sick again. By 'they', I guess she means Customs officials. I don't want to get Elif into any trouble! Which is why I have a document that will make everything okay.

"Look, I could hide back under the seat," I say quickly, telling her my Plan A, before I explain Plan B. "OR we could just pretend to be family!"

"What?" squeaks Elif, her voice high in surprise.

"Look!" I say, quickly pulling a folded A4 sheet out of my rainbow bag. "This is a letter from my mum – sort of – saying you're my big cousin and that she gives her permission for you to take me to the UK to see my father. I got the idea from Astrid doing it for Tiger."

"WHAT?!" Elif repeats even louder.

"It's fine! When I was staying in the office last night I wrote it on the computer, printed it out and copied my mum's signature on the bottom. And then I printed out this photo of the three of us together at the farm. It really looks like we're related! It'll be proof to the Customs people!"

I wave the printout of the photo that Kenzo – the Japanese student – took of us. On the computer

I zoomed in on Patti, me and Elif, cropping out half-a-dozen other people and two random goats.

I hear Elif mutter the German swear word again – and maybe one in Turkish – as she stares at all the paperwork. I quickly reach into the bag and pull out my own passport too.

"Me and you absolutely look alike! We can do this!" I assure her.

Elif looks as sick as I feel.

And now I'm aware that everyone is starting to come back to the car deck. The noise and the chatter is burbling around us, louder and louder.

"Oh, mein gott!" I hear Elif say with a weary sigh.

Then she grabs the papers and photos from my hand as the crunch of docking lets us know we're here. We've arrived. We're in Dover!

"Okay. I'll say you're my cousin. We'll use these documents," says Elif as we roll out of the ferry, down the ramps and get waved into one of the many queues for Customs. "I can't see how this will work, but it's better than them searching the van and finding you hiding."

"Yay!" I whoop.

Then, as relief hits me, so does the nausea.

"No! Nein!" I hear Elif say, and see her hand pointing towards my feet, where some crumpled empty plastic packets have been chucked.

I grab one gratefully, and for the next few minutes I mostly have my head in what was a family-size packet of Lays Poulet Roti (roast chicken) crisps as we roll up to a Customs booth.

I hear the squibbly-squeet of glass against rubber as Elif manually rolls down her window. Then I can vaguely make out her talking to the official-looking woman who is studying our documents.

"My cousin is a very bad traveller," Elif explains to her.

I raise my fingers and wiggle them feebly at the Customs person. The Customs person takes one look at me, wrinkles her nose as I throw up again, and waves us away.

I want to shout "YES!" at the top of my voice, but my tummy has other ideas, as I vomit my way into the UK . . .

MARGOT

Hey Diary,

I know I usually wait till bedtime to write, but I need to offload about something that happened about half an hour ago.

So I took Charlie to his swimming lesson at the leisure centre this afternoon (whoopee . . .) cos Mum and Dad had lots to do for us going away tomorrow. I sat at a table in the glass-walled cafe and kept half an eye on Charlie (though from where I was sitting, his 'swimming' lesson looked more like a divebomb-and-roar session). Anyway, at the same time, I was flicking through my socials and wondering why Marisa still wasn't getting back to me, when I heard someone say my name.

It was Destiny, who's in my year, and in the same Maths class as Marisa. She was wearing this cropped sports top in a deep purple, with matching leggings and white chunky, box-fresh trainers. Her long braids were in a ponytail and she had these cute kiss curls. She was holding a water bottle, her acrylics all new and glossy, on the way to the gym or a class here at the leisure centre. Honestly, I'm describing all this cos she could literally have been a backing dancer in a music video or something the way she looked so perfect. She also looked a lot older than me and fifty times cooler.

No way did I expect Destiny to acknowledge me; not cos she's, y'know, horrible in that popular-girl way, but just cos we don't really know each other and have nothing in common. Yeah, or so I thought . . .

Anyway, Destiny gives me a wave, says hi, and stops beside me. "Heard from Marisa?" she asks. I say no, wondering what she means, wondering if she even knows Marisa well enough to know she's gone on holiday. And then Destiny says, "Oh, wow, so you haven't seen what she posted last night?"

I'm pretty sure I know what socials Marisa is on, cos we're on the same ones, obviously! But all of a sudden Destiny's holding her phone in front of me, and it's Marisa and her sister Toni in tiny dresses, laughing and dancing in a club. In a club? I mean, Marisa's fourteen, same as me. (Same as Destiny, not that you'd guess that!) But how did Marisa manage to get into a club? And how come I hadn't seen this and Destiny had? What social's this even on?!

Then Destiny grins and says, "Marisa totally stole those moves from the Zumba class we went to last Tuesday!"

And that's when I found out that Destiny and I do have something in common – hanging out with Marisa. Who knew? Not me!!

And that was also the moment when Charlie flung himself at the other side of the glass wall from me, like a wet fish walloping against it, and mouthed "FINISHED!!". I was never so glad to see the little idiot. I quickly mumbled "Bye" to Destiny and got out of there.

So what exactly is going on with Marisa? Why does it suddenly feel like she's acting more like a stranger than a so-called best friend, Diary?

#Confused
#Ghosted

WANDA

I can't believe this.

I'm standing on the ACTUAL doorstep of my ACTUAL dad's house ACTUALLY ringing the doorbell!

I'm so excited that my heart feels like it's about to explode out of my chest.

Is that even possible, though? Can hearts explode? Immediately I picture a cartoon of a heart going KA-BOOM!! like something off 'Itchy and Scratchy' in The Simpsons. Ooh, maybe I saw that in one episode! I need to Google and see if—

"Hey, Wanda . . ." I hear Elif interrupt my mind's ramblings. She's standing beside me on the garden path of this totally ordinary house, nervously jangling her campervan keys. "Your father, he definitely knows you're coming, right? You called him, right?"

I WANT to say yes.

But I've used up my lying quota for the day (the week, the year, even.)

"No . . ." I mumble.

Suddenly I feel like I'm falling down a well in slow motion.

"Wanda!!" Elif groans. "What if he's not home?"

"I dunno . . ." I mumble.

I'm tumbling further down into the dark well, recognising that this is something I do all the time. I get an idea in my head that seems like THE BEST IDEA EVER! And then I run with it till I suddenly stop, not really sure what I'm supposed to do next.

I go from all the enthusiasm to not having zero per cent of a clue.

From all the energy to complete exhaustion.

And all my focus went into getting me here today, to standing on this doormat with 'Welcome' written on it. NONE of my focus went into thinking about what I'd do when my dad Lee opens the door. That's IF he opens the door.

Uh-oh; the overlapping conversations start jabbering in my overheating head . . .

- What if my dad is out at the supermarket?
- What if he's at work?
- What if he's gone on holiday for a week?
- What if he doesn't live here any more?
- He has to!
- But why should he?
- It's been more than twelve years since he scribbled his 'Love you, Patti' on the back of the photo in my bag – THAT'S why.
- What if he's emigrated to Australia? Or Dubai? Or Ecuador!
- OH, NO! HE MIGHT HAVE EMIGRATED TO AUSTRALIA OR DUBAI OR ECUADOR!!!
- Aaargh!!
- Help – what if a POLICEMAN lives here now?
- He'll open the door, take one look at me and know that I'm completely guilty of . . . I dunno . . . just being an awful, lying stowaway and he'll arrest me straight away.
- Okay, don't panic; I just need to get a Plan C.

- Plan C = me getting away from here fast.
- I need to turn around and run away right—

"Hello?" says an older man, opening the door.

He has pinky-pale skin, silvery-grey hair in a sort of quiff at the front, and a matching little bitty triangular beard on his chin. He's wearing a grey jumper with diamond shapes on it and jeans that have no shape. His glasses are black-rimmed and he's staring at me through them. All I can think is that his eyebrows are incredibly bushy, and they're bobbing up and down as he tries to figure out what a twelve-year-old girl and a sulky-looking young woman in her twenties are doing on his garden path.

"Yes? Can I help you, ladies?" the man tries again. He looks quite stern. Quite serious.

And he's obviously not my dad, Lee. But it doesn't mean Dad isn't here, does it?

Elif nudges me from behind, trying to push me to say something.

"Hello," I mutter. "Is Lee in?"

My words sound stupid. Like I'm asking if a kid is coming out to play.

"Lee?" the man says quizzically. "There's no one here by that name. I'm Paul Swanson, and I live here."

Oh no . . . this man clearly doesn't know my dad. This is BAD. My eyes start stinging, filling with tears.

"Wanda, what is this? You said this is the address for your father?" says Elif, sounding exasperated with me.

"It is! Or it was . . . Wait, I'll show you!" I say, scrabbling in my rainbow bag for the packet of photos.

"Hold on; what did you call her?" the man asks Elif.

"Her name is Wanda. She's trying to find her father, Lee," Elif replies, probably trying to speed things up, probably panicking that she's never going to get rid of me. "You haven't heard his name? You don't know where we could find him?"

The man is quiet for a second, then says, "When you say 'Lee' . . . you're not talking about my son Louis, are you, young lady?"

I have the packet. I'm pulling out the photo with the message. I glance back up at the man and see that he's scrunched up his face as he stares at me. And with his nose wrinkled like that, I can just make out his front teeth – and the gap between them! Same as mine! Same as Lee's in this photo! With fumbling fingers, I hold up the photo of Lee smiling his gap-toothed smile on that long, hot, forever-ago summer.

"Mr Swanson – look! Look at this!" I burst out. "It's my dad, Lee. And this is my mum, Patti; she was his girlfriend. They met backpacking around Greece years ago."

I scrabble around with the photos and hold up the picture of his son and my mum together.

The man looks shaken.

"I don't understand . . . How did you get Louie's photo? And why are you calling him 'Lee' . . . and 'Dad'? And why are you calling yourself 'Wanda'?"

"Because that's my name!" I say with a laugh. "I think – I mean, I'm pretty sure I'm your granddaughter!"

"Eh?" he mumbles, looking totally full of befuddlement. "What are you on about? I don't have a granddaughter; just a grandson . . ."

He's staring from one photo to another, and then he does a double take of me.

"Oh, my goodness!" he exclaims. "You're the spitting image of Louis!"

"I know!" I agree.

"My son is your father?!" he says, his voice cracking.

"YES!!" I burst out.

I feel like I'm glowing gold from the inside out.

I belong.

I belong here.

I belong to a family!

A family called Swanson!

Wow! If Patti and Lee had stayed together, I might have been Wanda Swanson instead of Wanda Bain. The kids at my old primary school in the UK called me Wanda No-Brain or Wanda Bird-Brain. They did it even when Mrs Chopra told them to stop. It was one of the millions of reasons Patti decided I should drop out of school and we'd go travelling and have a bunch of adventures instead. But maybe I'd've had different adventures if I'd been WANDA SWANSON! Maybe—

And then I see Mr Swanson wobble a bit, making a grab for the door frame. He might have crashed down right there and then, if me and Elif hadn't grabbed an arm each.

It was then that I wondered if I'd accidentally killed my brand-new grandfather with the shock of my existence.

MARGOT

Dear Diary,

Me again. This afternoon is getting more insanely awful by the second.

I HAVE BEEN OFFICIALLY DUMPED BY MY BEST FRIEND! I know!!!

So here's what happened. After Destiny dropped that bombshell at the leisure centre earlier, I saw some Snapchats that Marisa put up. She posted photos taken this afternoon; there she was on the back of a moped, waving as some older boy drove her along! I think it was her big cousin Rosario, but still. She didn't look like herself. She had a tiny bikini top on and teeny shorts and a ton of make-up. She wasn't my Marisa at all!

My head felt so messed up that I messaged her. I said that I'd bumped into Destiny, who'd shown me the mystery post of Marisa and Toni out clubbing. I asked which social it was on. Then I asked who the driver of the moped was. I also asked how come Marisa hadn't got back to any of my messages from the last couple of days. And then I asked what the deal was with going to Zumba at the leisure centre with Destiny last Tuesday, and how come I never knew about that. I mean, I said it all very friendly and everything.

But Marisa didn't seem to see it that way! She got back to me pretty much instantly, and I can't believe what she said . . . She said – get this – that I was sounding like a jealous boyfriend or girlfriend or something! As if?!

It didn't stop there.

She went on to tell me that back home we were together too much and that it was a bit too claustrophobic for her. That she wanted to hang out with other people sometimes, and what was the problem with that?

AND IT DIDN'T STOP THERE!

She said that I was always going on about my little brother and moaning about my grandad and that she wanted to have friends that were a bit more grown-up and fun, and that she was sorry – SORRY! – but she didn't think we should hang out any more.

So there I was, in total shock about what Marisa had just messaged me, and then Dad goes and calls me downstairs for an 'urgent family meeting', which consists of him asking me and Mum to use our phones to try and call his lost mobile and the equally lost landline handset. That way we could try and figure out where Charlie had hidden – and forgotten – both the phones for the last two days.

I felt like my head was about to explode, but I couldn't speak about Marisa right that second or I might've started crying and never stopped. So I just went along with it and bumbled around downstairs, listening out for the trill of a ringtone, while Mum went out in the garden. (Charlie used to bury things out there when he was really little – toothbrushes, spoons, nappies, Lego, bananas. I think he should've been a beagle rather than a boy.) Then I heard Mum shout that she thought she could hear a faint 'diddly-dee'-ing coming from up on the shed roof, so Dad went running out there, all excited. A few minutes later, I'd kind of got distracted (cos of everything) and forgotten what I was supposed to be doing. I was back scrolling, trying to spy on whatever Marisa was doing next – but all her photos were probably on the secret group she'd not bothered to tell me about.

And then I heard something really unexpected . . . Mum and Dad having a sort of hassled-sounding conversation out in the garden. An argument? It's really not like them; they're always sickeningly nice to each other. After sticking my head around the living-room door to check that Charlie was still glued to the Disney channel, I went and hovered in the kitchen doorway, trying to hear what was being said.

Mum was obviously upset, with this catch in her throat that made it hard for me to understand her. But it was stuff like, "I don't want your father to come with us!" and "Paul's going to spoil everything!" And Dad was going, "No, no, no! He doesn't mean anything by it, Gill! He'll be good, you'll see!" Then Mum was sniffling into Dad's shoulder and he was cuddling her and saying it would be all right, and that's when I thought they were coming back in, so I shot up here to write this stuff down.

Oh, hold on – the doorbell's just rung. If Mum and Dad are still talking in the garden, I'd better go answer it before Charlie does, or whoever's outside will be in for a bit of a surprise . . .

#EverythingIsRubbish

WANDA

Take Two: I'm standing on the ACTUAL doormat outside my ACTUAL DAD's house and my brand-new grandfather is ringing the doorbell.

I can't believe my luck . . . Lee/Louis/DAD lives just five minutes' drive from his childhood home, and he hasn't emigrated to Australia or Dubai or Ecuador or wherever. JOY!!! And I'm also lucky that my brand-new grandfather didn't collapse when he realised who I was, but took a) a deep breath, and b) control of the situation.

"Come on, hurry up . . ." my brand-new grandfather grumbles, pressing the doorbell again.

While we hover, something occurs to me.

"Excuse me, but what should I call you?" I ask him shyly.

"Eh?" he mutters, frowning round at me. "What do you mean?"

"Grandad? Grandpa?" I suggest.

"Um . . . Mr Swanson will do for now," he says simply, sounding even more stern and serious.

"Okay," I reply, trying to ignore the wave of disappointment bashing up against my chest. But sure, he's only known me twenty minutes. Having an instant granddaughter is a lot to take in. Maybe I'M a lot to take in . . .

Mr Swanson seems about to impatiently ring the bell again, when the front door is suddenly yanked open by a small boy wearing yellow swimming goggles on his head and nothing else.

Elif bursts out laughing. (I'm glad she's laughing. She hasn't been very happy with me since I got talking to my . . . er . . . Mr Swanson, and it became clear to her that I DIDN'T in fact know my dad, not even the teensiest bit, despite what I told her on the ferry. Oops.)

"What do you want?" asks the little boy very seriously.

I know who he is, thanks to Mr Swanson filling

me in on my dad's family – i.e. MY FAMILY!! – on the short drive here in Elif's van. The boy is Charlie, and he is four years old. He's the son of my dad and his partner Gill, WHICH MAKES HIM MY HALF-BROTHER!! Gill's daughter Margot lives here too. She's fourteen.

"Oh, for goodness' sake, Charlie, put some clothes on and get your parents!" Mr Swanson says gruffly, making his way inside the hallway. Me and Elif hesitantly follow him.

"Charlie's just chilling out after his swimming lesson, Pops," says a girl, bouncing barefoot down the carpeted stairs.

Margot.

She has straight, gingery red hair in a cute bob. I like her stripy T-shirt and denim shorts.

A little thrill shivers through me, as I suddenly realise that, technically, SHE IS MY STEPSISTER!

And now Margot's spotted us, she's looking warily at Elif first, and then me.

"What's going on, Pops?" Margot asks, as Mr Swanson takes his jacket off and hangs it on a peg by the door.

(She calls him 'Pops', not 'Grandfather'! That's cute!!)

"You'll find out in a minute, Margot," replies Mr Swanson.

"Paul?" comes a woman's voice from a room towards the back of the house. "What are you doing here? We weren't expecting you!"

As she comes into the hall, I see that the woman has the same red hair as the girl, only bundled back in a scruffy, stubby ponytail. She looks nice, but tired. She has to be Gill.

"We need an emergency family chat, Gill," says Mr Swanson, as my stepmum (MY STEPMUM!) frantically grabs a small top and shorts out of a pile of folded washing at the foot of the stairs and wrestles the little boy into them.

"Hello?" comes a following voice. "What's going on?"

It's a man, in a T-shirt, combats and trainers, carrying a phone handset that appears to be very dirty, like it's been left outside. It's even got some moss on it. Why does it have moss on it? And why is my ever-so-easily-sidetracked brain even BOTHERING to wonder why a handset is dirty and mossy when the important thing is the man holding it?

I give my head a shake and focus, because it's him.

HIM!!

He is smiling his gap-toothed smile.

He has a smattering of darker brown freckles across the light-brown skin of his nose.

He looks as friendly and beautiful as the photos of him in my bag, just a little bit older.

He is Lee Swanson and HE IS MY ACTUAL REAL LIVE DAD!!!

He gives me and Elif a confused nod hello.

"You've brought visitors, Dad?" my ACTUAL REAL LIVE DAD says to his own father. "You should've called!"

"Well, I did try, Louis, but you didn't answer the phone!" says Mr Swanson.

"Ah, yeah, we had a bit of a problem with it," says my ACTUAL REAL LIVE DAD, wiping the dirty handset with the bottom of his T-shirt and putting it down on a nearby table. "But you could've tried my mobile. Though, er, I'm not sure where that is, right now . . ."

"Well, there you go!" says Mr Swanson, like a judge, resting his case. "What was I meant to do?"

"Call my mobile, maybe?" Gill suggests, with a definite roll of her eyes.

Mr Swanson doesn't seem to notice.

"Or mine, Pops . . ." my stepsister (!) murmurs.

Margot thinks she said that so quietly that no one could've heard. But I heard her.

I hear everything when my nerves are jangling and raw. It's like my hearing becomes pin-sharp, my ears acting like hypersensitive spy satellites. Right now, I can hear the thrumming of traffic on the main road we drove along on our way here, even though it's streets away. I can hear electricity buzzing in a lamp on the hallway table. I can hear the dripping of a tap upstairs.

So I can definitely hear when a teenage girl says two whispered, sarky words to herself. But how come she's being sarcastic about her own 'Pops'?

"Sorry, there's been a bit of a mix-up with the phones and we can't remember where they were left," my dad apologises.

(What will HE want me to call him? 'Dad'? Or is it too soon for that as well? Would he prefer 'Lee'? Or 'Louis', maybe?)

"Well, can we at least all sit down for this?" says Mr Swanson, already heading into what must be the living room.

"Sit down for what?" asks Gill, but an answer never comes.

I don't know what order we're meant to go into the room. I don't think any of us know; we stare at each other, shuffle a bit and then Gill gives a puzzled smile and ushers me and Elif to go in first. Mr Swanson is standing with an elbow on the mantelpiece, a remote in his hand as he switches off the blaring TV. He nods for me to sit down on an armchair by the window, and Elif perches herself on the arm of it. Everyone else bumbles in and either sits on the sofa or the remaining armchair.

"So, does someone want to explain?" says my – eek! – dad.

"Well, I think *you've* got a bit of explaining to do, Louis!" says Mr Swanson. "Because it came as a shock to say the least when *this* pair turned up on my doorstep!"

Lee/Louis/my dad frowns, his eyes settling on me.

I smile at him.

He blinks.

He blinks his brown eyes that are the same as mine.

His skin flushes darker a little, especially around his sweet, sticky-out ears.

I think he's starting to understand, but isn't sure WHAT he's understanding.

Mr Swanson starts up again. "Well, it turns out that Elf here—"

"Elif," my friend tries to correct him, but he carries on regardless.

"—Elf here was working on a farm in France, picking fruit. She met a woman there called Patti and her daughter Wanda."

My dad's mouth falls open.

"Patti and Wanda have been travelling for several years now, staying in lots of different countries. Is that right, Wanda?"

I nod, fast – TOO fast, and make myself a bit dizzy.

"Anyway, it turns out that Wanda here didn't know who her father was, till she came across some information her mother had kept secret," Mr Swanson continues in his boomy voice, like he's the narrator in a play. "Then when Wanda's mother went away for a few days – to some hippy-dippy retreat – Wanda decided to stow away in Elf's campervan when she was leaving for England, and come to find him. Well, to find you, Louis."

"I did NOT know Wanda was in my van!" Elif quickly jumps in. "Not till we were already on the ferry. I'm supposed to be on my way to London by now. My cousins are expecting me!"

I don't think anyone's listening to Elif.

"Patti?" my dad murmurs, staring wide-eyed at me. "Patti Bain, you mean? She's your . . . mum?"

He's looking at me. Like properly looking. Trying to see Patti in my face, but seeing his mini-me instead.

"Patti . . . wasn't she that old girlfriend you told me about, Louis?" says Gill. "The one you met when you went travelling after university?"

My dad's partner doesn't seem angry, just a bit stunned. That makes me feel suddenly relieved. I hadn't thought till now that my dad could have a whole new family, and that little old ME turning up out of the blue might not be a particularly wowee-this-is-great surprise.

I quickly check out the girl and the little boy, to see their reactions. Margot's brown eyes are blink-blink-blinking at me. Charlie has wiggled his way across the floor on his bottom and is now sitting at my feet, gazing up at me open-mouthed, like I'm a yeti in a documentary about mythical creatures.

"Yes, she was!" I hear my dad answer Gill. "But I mean, we lost touch after I came back home – Patti wanted to stay out in Greece for a while longer. I had no idea . . . I mean, it's just that I didn't know she'd had a . . . that we'd had a . . ."

He can't quite say the word 'baby'.

But I can see he's now staring in shock at my top; Patti's ancient and faded Nirvana T-shirt, i.e. my look-a-like nightie. It looks cute with my leggings and trainers. I can't even remember putting it on this morning. This morning seems like ten years ago now.

"Oh, this was yours, I think?" I say, pulling at the hem of the T-shirt. "I've got a photo of you wearing it. I've got quite a few photos, actually, of you and my mum . . ."

I lean over towards the sofa, over Charlie's head, and hand them to my dad. Gill and Margot lean in to look at them too.

"You look so young, Dad!" Margot points out, with a little laugh in her voice, till she glances over at me and checks out the same T-shirt her dad is wearing in the photo, and a confused expression clouds her face again.

I realise my knee is being tapped.

"I don't really understand. Who ARE you?" Charlie cheerfully demands.

"I'm Wanda!" I say simply. I'll leave the part about me being his half-sister to his parents to explain in a four-year-old-friendly way.

"Why do you have the same name as our nana?" Charlie asks. "HER name was Wanda!"

(Wait – I'm named after a grandma I don't know? Lee's mother? How did that even happen?)

"I don't know," I say, shrugging, not sure how to explain anything any more. I think I've sort of stalled. "I don't know a lot of things . . ."

"This is all very well," Mr Swanson butts in. "And we can get into more of the details and reminiscing shortly. But first, we have to get practical. We have to phone this Patti, and tell her to get to the UK as quickly as she can."

"But like I told you, my mum's on a meditation retreat," I remind Mr Swanson.

"Yes, well, she'll have to stop with her meditating and come collect you," Mr Swanson carries on. "Now give me your mother's phone number, dear."

"Patti won't pick up – it's a silent retreat in some mountains," I try to explain. "Her phone's locked away till next Saturday. She thinks I'm at the farm, being looked after by her friend. She won't know I'm missing till then."

I spot my dad and Gill swapping raised eyebrow glances. That can't be good, can it?

"What? But that's another whole week away. And we're supposed to be going on our trip tomorrow!" says Mr Swanson, glancing round at his family. (Also MY family, I remind myself). "This is ridiculous!"

My eyes start to prickle. Is my brand-new grandfather saying me being here is ridiculous? I feel my happiness unravelling, and a squiggle of panic begin to wriggle in my chest.

"It's all right though! I wrote Patti a letter explaining everything and left it in our room at the farm," I say quickly. "As soon as she reads it she'll call me. Then she'll come for me!"

Mr Swanson is rubbing his hand on his head and

looking frustrated. "Well, Louis can phone this place she's staying and get hold of her. What's the name of the retreat?"

"I don't know!" I say, lying again.

Okay, I *might've* deliberately deleted the emergency number my mum inputted on my mobile . . .

"You!" says Mr Swanson, pointing at Elif. "You must have some contact details for Wanda's mother?"

Elif raises her hands. "I don't! I wasn't friends with Patti. I don't know anything about her plans! But I do know she loves Wanda, and will come for her straight away, once she gets the message."

That was nice of Elif to say, considering what she thinks of Patti. Which isn't much.

"Dad," my dad says to his own father. "Let's slow this down a bit, eh?"

"Yes, Paul, I think Wanda's getting a bit upset," says Gill.

"I don't mean to upset anyone; it's just that this must be one of those . . . what do you call them? Safeguarding issues!" says Mr Swanson, sounding more stern and serious than ever. Then he turns to me again. "Wanda, I'm sure you're a lovely girl, but you don't know us, and we don't know you, so for your own safety, I think the authorities will have to be involved."

"Social services, you mean?" says my dad, looking shell-shocked. "Is that really necessary?"

I feel Elif twitch next to me.

"Of course it's necessary! And as well as dealing with Wanda, they'll probably want to get in touch with the police here, who can liaise with the police in France, to help track down her mother," says Mr Swanson matter-of-factly. "Now Wanda's just a child—"

"I'm not a child, I'm twelve!" I try and say, but Mr Swanson just talks over me. I'm beginning to see why Margot sounded a bit sarky about him a few minutes ago.

"—and might not be able to give much information," he carries on, "but I'm sure Elf here can give them some details that could be helpful."

My skin has gone icy-cold.

This is all going horribly wrong . . . Am I going to be dragged away from my new family before I've even got to know them, even just the littlest bit?

I blink at my dad, who opens and closes his

mouth, like a startled goldfish.

"May I use your bathroom, please?" asks Elif, getting up from the arm of the chair I'm perched on.

"Sure, it's at the top of the stairs," says Gill, pointing back out into the hall.

"Thinking about it, Wanda, if you give us the name of the farm you're staying at this summer, that would be a start," Mr Swanson starts up again, taking a pen out of his jacket pocket as if he was a police officer about to take notes.

"I don't know! We all just called it 'the farm'!" I answer, hoping that seems believable, since Mr Swanson thinks of me as just some dumb 'child'. (And obviously, of course I know the farm's name . . . I'm just not about to tell him.)

"But you referred to it as an *eco*-farm, didn't you? Maybe I could try looking some of those up and—"

"Paul . . ." Gill says in a gentle-but-firm, please-give-it-a-rest sort of voice.

"Hey," my dad says brightly, all of a sudden. "Charlie, Margot . . . how about you take Wanda upstairs and show her your rooms, while we all have a chat down here?"

The hamster wheels in my head start rattling at MEGA-high speed.

- They're going to chat about ME, right?
- What is there to say?
- It won't be about how nice it is to have me here, that's for sure.
- How great that I came.
- It'll be about what to do with me.
- How to get rid of me as fast as they can.
- Didn't Mr Swanson say something about them all going on a trip tomorrow?
- They'll definitely want me out of the way, then.
- They'll want to talk more about calling the 'authorities', like Mr Swanson said.
- Maybe my dad and Gill and Mr Swanson won't even chat – maybe they want me out of the room to make the call!
- But what'll happen exactly?
- When will 'they' come for me?
- Who even are 'they'?
- Where will I go?

- And who'll take me there?
- Will my dad even know where it is?
- How will Patti ever find me if I'm not here?

"C'mon!" says Charlie, scrabbling to his feet and grabbing my hand. He tugs me towards the living room door and into the hall. Wordlessly, Margot falls in behind us, while urgent, hissed conversations start up before the living-room door's even been closed behind us.

Next, I find myself being enthusiastically pulled up the stairs by Charlie, who's saying something about sharks for some reason.

Then BOOM!, he kicks a door open and I'm in a cross between an aquarium and the soft toy aisle of a kid's department in a store. All four walls are painted as an undersea scene, with different types of sharks swimming around. Under the window there's a mound of little and large soft toy sharks on what I'm guessing is a bed.

"Cool room . . .!" I mumble, awestruck despite what's just happened downstairs.

My younger self would be madly jealous of this.

I'm madly jealous NOW! I've tried having collections of stuff before, but whenever I do, Patti always smiles sadly and says it's not a good idea, cos we're always moving around and need to travel light. It's why I collect foreign words and emergency numbers and stuff instead.

"Do you like sharks? I LOVE sharks!" says Charlie, jumping up on the pile of toys and starting to bounce, bounce, bounce, shouting, "I LOVE SHARKS! I LOVE SHARKS! I LOVE SHARKS!" like a tuneless chant.

"He's always like this," says a voice, and I turn to see Margot come into the room and lean her back against the closed door. "He'll stop in a minute when he gets bored."

"Okay," I mumble shyly.

"So . . . this is pretty weird, huh?" says Margot, with a little wry smile.

"Yeah, kind of," I agree, thinking for a second that she means the crazy, amazing room and the little boy in it.

But then I realise she's talking about ME turning up, and my heart sinks with worry again.

Especially since my spy-satellite hearing has tuned into something happening just outside Charlie's bedroom.

The flush of a loo from the bathroom close by. The squeak of a door. Feet padding downstairs. The soft swoosh of the front door being opened and quietly clicked shut. And then the rattling growl of an old campervan driving away into the distance.

I guess I can't blame Elif for sneaking off, for not getting involved, for not wanting to get into trouble with 'the authorities' cos she sort of smuggled a kid into the country.

But now, surrounded by sharks and strangers I don't know, I've never been so alone . . .

MARGOT

*Okay, Diary, so the most OMG thing ever, ever, **EVER** just happened today!*

Like right now, there is a total stranger brushing her teeth in our bathroom!!

And in about a minute that total stranger is going to be sleeping next door to me, in Mum's office, on the airbed that Dad is inflating.

I don't have time to write down everything that's gone on; Mum's shouting at me to get the spare duvet cos she's chasing Charlie around cos he won't go to bed cos it's all too crazy here.

*So all I'm going to say is that the total stranger who turned up at the door is actually – wait for it, Diary – my **SECRET SISTER**.*

I know, right?!
#OMG
#OMG
#OMG x100 . . .

MONDAY

WANDA

The kitchen smells of warm laundry and coffee.

"Morning, Wanda!" says Gill, smiling up at me from where she's crouching down, dragging clothes out of the tumble dryer. "Did you sleep okay?"

"Mmm," I say shyly.

I slide into the chair Margot's just pulled out for me around the small table. Charlie is sitting opposite, with his mouth full of cereal. He waves a milky spoon at me. Lee's not here, but I heard the sound of a shower running when I passed the bathroom on the way downstairs.

BTW, I've decided to think of my dad as 'Lee', just for now. If I call him 'Dad', even just in the privacy of my own head, it'll hurt more if I have to leave with someone from the 'authorities' today . . .

"That's good," says Gill, starting to fold up sheets. "It was a long day for you yesterday, Wanda. A lot to process."

Even if I'm still not sure what's going to happen to me, I do feel a weensy bit better after a night's sleep. Though it turned out to be way more than a night; it was like my whole system overheated and shut down for about 16 hours. (My brain does feel like a malfunctioning computer quite a lot of the time. Pretty sure I've got a faulty hard drive.) When Margot came to get me up a little while ago, she told me what had happened. Yesterday, in Charlie's room, I'd sat down on his bed of sharks, cos he wanted to tell me all their individual names. Margot noticed that while Charlie droned on about Diesel and Cheetos and Eddy and Oreo and whoever, my eyes started to close, then apparently I slowly slid sideways and zonked out among Charlie's cuddlies for HOURS. I looked like I was dead, she said. She had to stop Charlie from poking me with a felt-tip pen to see if I was still alive.

Then there was a hazy half-awake time where

Gill helped me up off the squished sharks and handed me some PJs that weren't mine. I bumbled behind her to a small, office room with a blow-up bed on the floor, and through my fug of exhaustion, I vaguely remember Charlie hurrying in and giving me one of his sharks (Oreo). Before I zonked again, I managed to grab Teddy Theo out of my rainbow bag too, which had appeared magically by my side, and then saw the outline of Lee saying "Night-night" in the doorway.

In the dark there, as I slept on the wobbly airbed, I dreamt I was back on churning sea, on the ferry, running in huge ship-shaped circuits around the decks, trying to avoid the police, trying to find Patti . . .

"What do you fancy for breakfast, Wanda?" Gill asks cheerfully. "Have whatever you want!"

The kitchen table has lots of stuff on it. Toast and peanut butter and two types of cereal and granola and some apple juice and orange juice and milk and croissants and plates and bowls and glasses.

I look at it all and feel frozen.

I'm starving, since I didn't eat yesterday. But I can't squash my brain into the right shape to make a decision, so I just sneak a peek at what Margot is having – a croissant and OJ – and copy her.

"Thanks." I smile at Gill.

My brain is so, SO weird. Weirdly wired, I mean. When it comes to small, ordinary, everyday stuff I can get myself in a total tangle over it and then give up and not bother doing anything at all. Like there was one time in Italy when Patti asked me to get a packet of pasta from the corner shop, and my head practically MELTED with twelvety billion questions and worries on the three-minute walk there:

- Have I got enough money?
- Did Patti give me too little by accident?
- She said to get farfalle, didn't she?
- Or did she say fusilli?
- Whichever, it's the one that's bow-shaped.
- Or did she mean the twisty one?
- Isn't the twisty one called penne, though?
- Uh-oh . . . how big a bag did she want me to get anyway?
- What if there's lots of sizes?
- How much do all the sizes cost?

- And what if the person at the till speaks to me?
- What might they say?
- What if they say something but speak too fast for me to understand?
- How do I say, *"Sorry, I don't really know many words in Italian"* in Italian?
- What if I hold everyone up in the queue at the till and they all get cross with me?

In the end, I was so stressed that I only got as far as the bread aisle, then turned around, went back to the flat and told Patti that the shop was completely out of pasta.

"Wanda, did you know that sharks don't have bones?" I suddenly hear Charlie ask.

I notice there's something else that's on the table, apart from breakfast stuff. It's a book about sharks. Charlie has it open at two pages that have all the different types of sharks there are, with their names underneath.

"Wow, no, I didn't!" I answer, curiosity making me forget to be worried for a second. "What're their skeletons made of, then?"

"Ooh, Charlie'll love you for taking an interest,

Wanda!" Gill says brightly. "We're all sharked out, aren't we, Margot?"

Margot grins and nods.

"Cartilage! Like the bendy bit here!" Charlie answers me enthusiastically, pressing the end of his nose with his finger. "So is it true that you hid away inside a van and came all the way from France?"

"Sorry, Wanda!" says Gill. "He's always changing direction when he talks!"

"Either that or he's always interrupting," Margot chips in, with a wry smile.

"I don't mind," I say honestly. "My mum says I do that all the time too. She says—"

"Sounds exciting!" Charlie interrupts. "Like when people stow away on pirate ships in stories!"

"It was only a tiny bit exciting," I tell him. "Hiding in the van was mostly really, really uncomfortable and very boring. And there were no pirates on the ferry. Just mums and dads and kids like you."

"Boo!" says Charlie. "And Pops said you've lived in lots of different countries with your mummy?"

"Yes," I reply, nodding. "Lots."

"Did you have to go to heaps of different schools

all the time? Did they talk different languages?"

"I don't go to school," I answer Charlie's question. "Well, not since me and my mum started travelling."

"NO SCHOOL!" Charlie practically yelps, jumping out of his seat and spilling what's left of his bowl of cereal and milk. "Mum, can I not go to school any more?"

"Nope, that's not happening, Charlie," says Gill, dropping her bundle of laundry on the counter and quickly grabbing some kitchen roll to wipe away Charlie's soggy mess.

"But Wanda doesn't have to! That's not fair!"

"It's just the way it is, darling!" says Gill, looking like she's clenching her jaw tight, I suddenly notice.

"NO SCHOOL! NO SCHOOL! NO SCHOOL!" Charlie sing-songs as he skips around the table.

"Think he's a bit overexcited, having you here," Margot leans over and says, as she takes a bite of her croissant.

"Sure, I get it," I reply to her.

Of course I get it. I've got madly excited and not known how to press the pause button about a million times. (A million times a day.)

"So what do you do if you don't go to school, Wanda?" asks Charlie, carrying on with his skipping. Gill leans over and expertly grabs his milk-dribbly spoon out of his hands.

I think for a second. It depends on where we're living. When Patti was waitressing at a beach cafe in Ibiza, I helped clean tables if I was in the mood, and I'd go collect shells and make them into patterns on the sand if I wasn't. Some places I made friends with stray cats, or watched people parasailing, or made ramps up steps for lizards, or read falling-apart books left behind by backpackers passing through.

I thought, since it was easier, I'd just tell Charlie about what I did this summer.

"Well, at the farm, I took turns laying out the plates and stuff for mealtimes, and I swam in the pond by the pine trees, and I fed and brushed the goats and—"

"Going swimming and petting goats sounds really good!" Charlie bursts out. "MUCH better than going to school!"

"Yeah, but—"

I'm about to mention that I try and do a bit of

English and maths online every day, but he's about to change subjects again.

"Urgh!" he mutters, stopping his manic skipping and coming to a halt beside me. "You smell of icky smoke, Wanda!"

I'm a bit shocked, then get what he might be talking about. I'd changed out of my borrowed PJs this morning back into my mum's well-worn Nirvana T-shirt. But now that I grab up a handful of the fabric and sniff it, I can see what he means.

"Two days ago, there was a fire at the farm where I live," I explain. (How can it be only two days ago? Doesn't it feel like six weeks since that happened? Time's gone *bendy* . . .) "All my stuff got the smoke smell in it."

"A FIRE? What KIND of fire?!?" Charlie asks wide-eyed.

"Not a big one," I say quickly, trying to get his excitement levels down before he gets too manic. It's like I can sense the adrenaline levels rising in his system. "Someone accidentally dropped a candle on a beanbag. It was only a little fire but it made a bad smell."

"Did the fire engines come?" asks Charlie.

"Yeah, one came, but I'd already put the fire out."

Charlie is looking at me as if I am Spiderman and a whole bunch of other superheroes rolled in one.

"YOU put the fire out? How?"

"I just grabbed a garden hose from outside and pointed it into the barn," I try and clarify. "It wasn't a big deal.

"Sounds pretty big!" says Margot, looking properly impressed.

Now Charlie is staring hard at me, and I'm expecting another fire-related question. But he off-roads again.

"Wanda, are you coming on holiday with us today?"

And there it is, my heart and tummy and hopes all crushed together in a lift that is instantly plummeting down to the basement. They're all going away, on a trip, like Mr Swanson said yesterday.

So what happens to me? Is this where Gill starts speaking about social services getting involved? Is someone official on their way around RIGHT NOW, to take me away?

"Yes, Charlie! Wanda is coming on holiday with

us today," Lee announces, walking into the kitchen at the PERFECT moment, beaming his mega-watt, gap-toothed smile. My heart, tummy and hopes start rising in the lift again.

"YAY, YAY, YAYYY!!" yelps Charlie.

"Oh, that's great!" says Margot, clapping her hands together.

"Do you want to explain things to Wanda?" says Gill, staring intently at Lee.

"Sure," he says, pulling out a chair and grabbing himself some toast to butter.

When Lee kicks off with his explanation I have to concentrate *really* hard, because my head is FULL of bubbles of excitement and rushing waves of relief, and all that extremely LOUD internal noise almost drowns him out.

"To be fair to your grandfather, Wanda, technically he's right. I mean, it probably *is* a safeguarding issue, having you here when we don't properly know each other, even if we *are* related," Lee starts off. "But Gill and I talked it over after he left last night, and it didn't sit well with us, to have you possibly taken into temporary foster care, I mean. So the deal is, we all go on our trip to the farm holiday cottage today, and if you give me your mum's phone number, I'll keep trying to get hold of her. We're booked at the farm till Friday, and it's only about an hour away from Dover, so if she picks up her messages earlier, we can get back home really quickly. But if worst comes to worst, and she doesn't get our voicemails till Saturday, then I'm sure – as you've said – she'll get here as soon as she can. Which'll be Sunday, I guess. How does that sound?"

HOW DOES THAT SOUND?!

I absolutely *love* the 'if worst comes to worst' part. That would give me seven whole days with Lee. HOW ACE IS THAT!!

I'm kind of aware that he's saying something else, something about how we might have to think again if Patti doesn't get in touch as planned next weekend. But I'm ignoring that because it's all good and everything is brilliant and I am going on ACTUAL HOLIDAY WITH MY ACTUAL FAMILY!

MARGOT

Dear Diary,

We are nearly at Badgers Bottom Farm (!! I know).

Sorry if my handwriting is scrappy and awful, but I'm writing this in the back of the car, and since we turned off the motorway the road's been really bumpy. I would say that Pops is going to freak out driving his beloved car down here (the one he washes and polishes practically every day!) but oops, he isn't coming on our family trip after all!

He's sulking.

Yep, that's right, my sixty-two-year-old grandad is sulking.

I don't know exactly what was said yesterday in the living room – cos me and Charlie were upstairs trying to entertain/get to know our surprise guest – but it turned out that Dad actually stood up to Pops. Shock! He never does that. Mum came into my bedroom later and said that Dad was very respectful and everything, but told Pops that he didn't feel comfortable getting social services involved. It sounded too scary for Wanda to handle, he told Pops, to be alone when she had come so far to meet him. And Dad had made up his mind that Wanda was going to stay with us till her mum came for her.

Pops got in a total strop, apparently. He was already mad that the campervan girl had vanished. "Has she got something to hide?!" Pops had wondered aloud, but I just thought that Elf (Elif?) sounded like she was a bit shocked at having a stowaway on board, and didn't much enjoy being bossed about by a man she didn't know who seemed to be about to land her in a lot of trouble with the police or whoever. I reckon if I was Elf/Elif, I'd've tiptoed out the door and legged it too . . .

Then Mum told me that Pops sighed and said it was a pity that we'd now have to give up our farm mini-break, and Dad had said, "Why? We'll just take Wanda with us till we figure things out!". Apparently, that was when Pops announced that he had nothing more to say and was going to leave. And because Pops always has something more to say, before he actually left, he stopped long enough to tell Dad that a) he wasn't going to come on holiday with us if Dad was going to be 'so ridiculous', and b) to get back in touch with him when Dad had come to his senses, and Pops would be only too glad to help out then.

When Mum let me know all of that, she was practically punching the air. She loved my nana, and used to quite like Pops, but he's so full-on now Nana's gone that he wears Mum down. He wears us all down!

But back to yesterday: it was all v. strange. Once Wanda's friend snuck off, Wanda went totally quiet and fell asleep for HOURS on Charlie's bed. As if someone just took her batteries out! So she missed the excitement of Pops storming out. She missed me, Mum and Dad trying to make sense of what happened, while Charlie sat in front of 'Shark Tale', which is his favourite movie ever.

After that, Dad blew up an airbed in Mum's office for Wanda. She seemed barely awake when we all led her through from Charlie's room last night. I lent her a pair of my PJs and made sure her cute rainbow bag was right by her side, in case she needed anything from it. Charlie was so sweet; he gave Wanda one of his soft toy sharks to keep her company.

But all through that, she just seemed pretty out of it. I guess it was a big day for her. I mean, if it was huge for me and Mum and Dad and Charlie (Dad having another, unexpected, unknown kid! I KNOW!!), can you imagine what it was like for Wanda?

This morning she was totally different, though. Well, she was quiet at first at breakfast, but then as soon as Dad said she was coming with us on holiday she just sort of lit up! She started telling us all these stories about herself and she has had SUCH an amazing life! Mine's been completely boring compared to Wanda's, even though I'm two years older than her. I can't wait to hear loads more about all the places she's been and the interesting people she's met. While she's been travelling around with her cool mum, it feels like I've just been mostly stuck at home, going to school and hanging out with my one – and it turns out useless – friend!

And speaking of my ex-best friend . . . So this absolutely massive thing has happened to me and my family, right? And I bet this news would completely blow Marisa's mind. But it's more fun to think I'm keeping it all to myself. Marisa doesn't deserve to share this excellent bit of gossip. She can just take all her silly selfies in Sicily, in tons of make-up and tiny amounts of clothes, while I'm here having an actual, amazing, life-changing moment.

Uh-oh – Mum has just pointed out the farm sign to Charlie, and he's going mad, practically bouncing off his seat in between me and Wanda.

And now Wanda is waking up, after zzz-ing all the way here.

And here – at the ridiculously named Badgers Bottom Farm – is where it all properly starts.

Where I get to know my stepsister.

How wild is that?

#TakeThatMarisa

#ICanHaveSecretsToo

#SecretsThatAreABillionTimesBetterThanYours

WANDA

"BADGERS BOTTOM FARM!! YAYYYYY!!!"

Charlie's yell startles me awake, making me sit bolt upright till I realise a seatbelt is holding me down.

It takes a few seconds for my heart rate to calm down from 'AAAARGHHHH!' to 'oof'.

"We're going to have the BEST time ever, Wanda!" Charlie practically whoops in my face. "We're going to pet and feed and love ALL the animals!"

"Uh-huh," I agree, trying to wake up and get my bearings.

And here's where I am – in a car, with Lee, Gill, Margot and Charlie, turning into a yard full of a muddle of nicely painted outbuildings.

LEE and GILL and MARGOT and CHARLIE – how

nuts does that sound?! I didn't know any of them till about 4pm yesterday!

And another thing; when I left the farm in France yesterday morning, I didn't exactly expect I'd be arriving at ANOTHER farm today. But that's just what happens when you accidentally come on holiday with the family you didn't know you had . . .

"Are you okay, Wanda?" Lee turns to me from the passenger seat and asks.

At least I THINK that's what he's asking. Charlie is chanting "BADGERS BOTTOM! BADGERS BOTTOM! BOTTOM BOTTOM BOTTOM BOTTOM!!!" at the top of his voice, right in my left ear. So I just nod at Lee and hope it's the right response.

But the funny thing is, a little part of me is a bit disappointed that this trip is happening. Just a teeny bit, I mean. It's just that I'd pictured myself hanging out in a regular house for once. One with a living room and a kitchen and a bedroom you didn't have to share with a ton of other people. I haven't been in a regular house like that for three years. MORE than that, really; me and Patti often used to live in rooms in other people's flats when I was growing up.

The only regular house I've known was my gran's. It smelt of onions a lot of the time (why, why, WHY did Gran cook everything with onions?), but it was still normal and ordinary and lovely in a normal, ordinary, onion-y way.

"There's our one – Barn Owl Cottage!" says Lee, and Gill turns and parks in front of a farm building that might have been a grain store or a stable or piggery once upon a time. Now, it has a duck-egg blue front door with a brass owl doorknocker and tweedy checked curtains at the windows. I'm suddenly excited to know what a holiday cottage is like. (Me and Patti and Gran used to stay in an old caravan when we went to Ireland when I was younger.)

I find out pretty quickly after we all spill out of the car and take the jumble of luggage inside. Barn Owl Cottage is TOTALLY GORGEOUS. The front door opens into a brilliant space; a living room with fat, squashy sofas, a gigantic TV (a TV!!) and other rooms off that which are just for the five of us. (I'm one of FIVE – how nuts is that?)

"Do you want *this* one or *that* one?" asks Margot, pointing to the two single beds in a room that has carpet so thick my feet sink into it like I'm stepping on CLOUDS. Both beds look luscious. The duvets are all puffy and the pillows are piled high.

"I'll have that one, please," I say, like I care which floofy bed will be mine. I drop myself and my rainbow bag down onto to it, and it practically *boings* me back onto my feet! The bed I shared with Patti in the loft room at the eco-farm had a mattress that was so thin I could feel as well as hear the squeaky metal bed springs every time I turned.

Margot chucks her barrel bag down on the floor by the other bed and tucks her bobbed and nutmeggy-red hair behind her ears.

"You've done me a favour," she says. "I was supposed to share with Charlie, but now you're here, he's in Mum and Dad's room, on a sofa bed."

I don't have great memories of sofa beds. I shared one with Patti when we lived for a while with a friend of hers in Budapest. I was supposed to go to sleep on it when Patti and her friend were still sitting at the table nearby drinking wine and playing guitar and singing songs together. (Patti said they always chose quiet Hungarian folk songs, but even if that's not exactly as loud as grime or punk or something, it's still pretty hard to go to sleep when people are yodelling sadly a few feet away.)

"How about we go and explore?" Margot suggests, pointing towards the French doors I hadn't spotted up till now. "If we go out this way, Charlie won't notice we're gone and try to come with us . . ."

I like Charlie a LOT, and yeah, I feel a bit mean skipping out on him, but the chance to hang out with my cool, older stepsister – just us! – is too amazing.

So I find myself following Margot out into a cobbled area, with more duck-egg blue front doors and prettily named buildings to the left and right of us. Ahead, across the cobbles, is the bright green of a field full of these little wooden pod things. There's also a tall wooden post with signs pointing off it.

"Pops was meant to be staying in one of those little shepherd's huts," says Margot, pointing to the pods, as we walk in that direction.

"How come he changed his mind?" I ask.

Okay, so I'm pretty sure it was something to do with ME upsetting plans. I could hear snippets of words, of raised voices downstairs when I was sitting on Charlie's bed of sharks yesterday afternoon. After my wild day, I think the stress of the spiky voices was the last straw. I think *that* probably made me shut down and close off.

But actually, maybe I *shouldn't* have asked Margot to confirm that I've messed up her – OUR – grandfather's holiday plans. Maybe I don't need to hear that.

"Oh . . . that's just the way Pops is," Margot answers vaguely, which makes me think she knows more than she's saying. "He's just really grouchy these days. He's been like that since Nana died."

"Your nana was Wanda!" I remember, still surprised to find my name came from *somewhere*, rather than being something that just randomly occurred to Patti, like she told me.

"Yeah, Nana Wanda!" Margot turns, hitting me with this sunshine smile that lights up her face. "Last year she'd really wanted to go travelling around the West Indies, where her family came from. Pops was the manager of this big DIY store, but he retired early, so they could do that. But then Nana got sick and died. And he's just . . . *angry* with everything now.

He's such a grouch. You probably noticed!"

I instantly picture Mr Swanson with a clipboard, ticking important things off important lists as he marches up and down aisles of tools and paint and stuff, while loads of staff in hi-vis uniforms say things like, "I'll get on to that right away, Mr Swanson!". Then I picture my grandfather with his hands in his pockets, staring out of his living-room window, all on his own and not knowing what to do with himself.

"I bet it's bit scary for him," I say aloud.

"Huh?" says Margot.

"Well, I guess he was in control at work, and now he doesn't have that," I explain. "Then he couldn't control your nan getting ill . . . I think that's why it must be kind of scary for him."

Margot doesn't say anything for a few seconds, then mutters, "Wow – I hadn't thought of it that way! I guess I always just think adults know what they're doing. Specially old ones like Pops!"

Oh, they don't . . . I think to myself, picturing all the grown-ups I've met along the way. And grown-ups are who I've hung out with over the last few years, since most backpackers don't have children kicking along with them. When I think of grown-ups sometimes being a bit clueless, I guess I'm thinking most of all of my mum. I'm starting to think Patti never knows what she's doing, and is just making it up as she goes along . . .

"So, what do we want to check out?" I hear Margot say, as we get to the wooden signpost. "Sheep? No. Pigs? No, thank you. Goats? Nope. Pond, Barbeque, Firepit and Games Room? NOW you're talking!"

Margot sets off to the right, and I bounce along beside her, happy to be with her, happy to be wearing the T-shirt and denim skirt and comfy Crocs she's lent me, along with a whole bag of other nice stuff back in the cottage. This is SO much more fun than waiting endlessly for Patti to finish work in the fields, trying to pass the time doing online lessons I don't really understand on the creaky, old computer in the eco-farm office.

"Oh, wow!" says Margot, as we come across a small but beautiful pond, with decking beside it.

On the deck there are three or four deckchairs and a stand with a red-and-white life ring attached to it. In the pond itself, a duck and its babies busily bustle around. It's perfect. If I had a swimsuit with me, I'd change into it and go swimming among the ducklings right now . . .

"Check this out!" I hear Margot say.

She's a little way away, leaping from one chunk of tree trunk to another, her green Converse landing with a soft *thud, thud*. The circular chunks are roughly spaced out and placed as seating around a firepit that's filled with ashes and burnt bits of wood.

"Hey, we can come up one night and toast marshmallows!" Margot suggests.

"I've never done that before!" I say, walking over to join her.

The old burnt smell from the firepit makes me shudder. I mean, it smells a *lot* nicer than burnt fabric and melted polystyrene balls, but I don't want to see another fire again in a hurry.

But then again, if the fire in the barn hadn't happened, I literally wouldn't be standing here, with my newly discovered stepsister, would I?

"Come on – let's see what's in there!" says Margot, now pointing at a long, low wooden building with double doors popped open. A handmade sign saying

'Games Room' is dangling off a nail at an angle.

I follow Margot as she hurries towards it, thinking that the building was probably once a barn, same as the one back in France.

"Yessss!" Margot hisses happily as she flips the light switch just inside the entrance and we see a netted ping-pong table in front of us to the left, and a green-felted pool table to the right. As well as that there's a darts board on the far wall and some beat-up sofas around a low coffee table.

"Come on – how good a shot are you?" asks Margot, passing me a dart.

I've never played darts before. I don't know what all the red and black rings and numbers mean. But I know aiming for the centre is a good idea.

"So your mum went out with my dad . . ." says Margot, as I get ready to throw the dart. "I still can't get my head around that."

"Neither can I," I say, as I let go of the dart and see it thwack into the wall, a couple of feet away from the board itself.

Margot bursts out laughing. Bursting out laughing is good; it makes me do the same. And if I do the same as Margot I'll fit in, I'll be fine. Everyone will think I know what I'm doing. (Ha!)

"I'm really glad you're here, Wanda," says Margot, tapping the toe of her green trainer against one of my/her borrowed Crocs.

"Me too." I grin shyly back.

This feels good, hanging out with her, just us. We can find out SO much about each other over the next few—

"Hello?"

We turn and see two girls, hovering in the doorway. They're practically identical. Twins, definitely, though one looks slightly taller than the other. They're both in short-shorts and sliders, with vest tops in different pastel colours. They've got their shiny dark hair scraped back in smooth ponytails, and both have sunglasses perched on their heads.

"Hi!' says Margot.

"Hi!" I copy her quickly, including the hand she's holding up to them, waving a quick hi.

"You just arrived? We saw you parking up outside Barn Owl Cottage," says the taller of the girls, coming in and leaning against the back of the sofa. "We're in the biggest place on the farm, Golden Eagle Cottage."

"We've been here all week. It's pretty boring," says the slightly shorter girl, padding over to join her sister. "Mum and Dad think we're still six and not sixteen, and don't get that we're not interested in coming to places like this any more."

"Yeah, totally," says Margot, with a nod.

"Totally," I mumble.

"But we're going home on Wednesday," the taller one adds. "And at least we've got a hot tub . . ."

"Uh, wow!" says Margot. "Yeah, we haven't got one of those."

"Nope," I agree, while trying to picture what a hot tub is and what it's for.

"Yeah, anyway, I'm Esha and this is Samira," says the taller sister.

"Sam," says the shorter one.

The twins are sixteen, I register them saying. A couple of years older than Margot. A whole lot older than me.

"So I'm Margot, and this is . . ." Margot pauses in her introduction and grins at me. "Well, it's complicated!"

We both laugh at our in-joke, our shiny new secret.

Which feels AWESOME.

"How come it's complicated?" asks the twin who is Esha, staring at us both.

"Well, it's a funny story," Margot begins.

Actually, I'm not sure I'm ready for her to share our story with anyone else quite yet. But before Margot can say anything, I hear a whole bunch of frantic quacking, like the duck family are being attacked by wolves!

"What's that?" says Margot.

"Oh, is there a little kid with you guys?" asks Sam. "We saw a boy just now throwing crisps at the ducks."

Okay, so crisps aren't the ideal nutritional food for ducks. But it sounds like there's something more worrying going on out at the pond than ducklings pecking at salt and vinegar crisps.

I start running.

And when I burst outside, I see three things . . .

1) A pile of age-4 clothes on one of the deckchairs by the pond.

2) An empty crisp packet bobbing on the water.

3) A boy in his pants wading into muddy water that's about to get too deep for him.

"Charlie! What are you doing?" I hear Margot yell behind me.

I'm kicking off the orange Crocs she lent me.

"I just wanted to stroke the ducklings!" says Charlie, turning around, wobbling quite a bit. The water's already up to his chest.

I've unbuttoned my skirt, let it drop to the grass and step out of it.

"Well, get out of there now!" Margot orders him.

"I can't – it's all sticky and sucky on my feet," says Charlie, with an edge of panic in his voice.

The cold of the water makes me gasp as I wade in. The mud at the bottom of the pond is definitely pretty sticky and sucky. But in about a nano-second I've got close enough to wrap my arm around Charlie's waist and I'm yanking him out of the pond and depositing him up on the decking for Margot to deal with.

"Oh, Charlie! You moron!" says Margot, with concern in her voice as she dries to dry him off with his T-shirt. "What did you think you were doing? You can't even swim properly yet! That was so dangerous!"

"But the ducks were so cute and it's not fair cos

WANDA gets to play in a pond back in France!"

As I pull myself out of the pond, I can hear the pad of feet running, and the worried voices of Gill and Lee calling out Charlie's name.

And I can hear something else too. Sniggering. Esha and Sam are looking me up and down and hiding grins behind their hands.

I look down at myself – and I get it.

My knickers are full of pond water and are hanging like a full nappy. And my borrowed white T-shirt has gone see-through now that it's wet, and what the twins are seeing is the fact that I'm not wearing a bra, even though I'm clearly starting to need one.

It's on Patti's list to get sometime (never), along with new PJs . . .

MARGOT

Hey Diary,

While everyone's busy, I thought I'd hang out in my room – mine and Wanda's room! – and write down some stuff.

So this morning's been pretty interesting so far!

First, we met these twin sisters who are here on holiday too. They're called Esha and Sam. They're here for another two days, so maybe me and Wanda can hang out in the barn with them in the evenings, instead of playing games with Charlie or watching boring Charlie-friendly kid movies.

And, speaking of Charlie, he was such an idiot earlier. For a start, he'd come looking for me and Wanda but didn't bother telling Mum or Dad where he was going. So of course they totally freaked out when they realised the front door of the cottage was open and he was nowhere to be found. Then he completely forgot about us when he spotted some ducklings in the pond. It might have been fine if he'd just watched them, but no, no . . . Charlie being Charlie, he takes off his clothes and goes right into the pond. He could've drowned! I mean, he's only had three swimming lessons so far.

Just as well that Wanda was amazing. Before it had really dawned on me what was happening, she was right in the water, dragging my stupid, darling brother out.

Anyway, drama over, Mum and Charlie are all cuddled up on the sofa watching 'Shark Tale'. And Dad and Wanda; well, after she got dried off and changed, Dad decided it would be good if him and her went for a drive to the supermarket in the town nearby, to shop for food for the next few days.

I guess it's cos Dad wants some getting-to-know-each-other time with Wanda, just him and her. Or maybe he's got specific questions about her mum or something. I totally get it, I really do, but it felt a bit weird watching them drive off; like this stranger, this unknown girl, is getting to hang out with my dad. And I guess that's what is really weird about it – in a way, she's more his daughter than I am . . .

But that's just me being silly. Wanda is really nice. Wanda rescued Charlie!! So it's all good.

Will write more later, like usual, at bedtime.

#WandaWonderWoman!

WANDA

Lee swings the car out of the entrance to Badgers Bottom Farm and onto the road that will take us towards the town nearby.

I can see our route on the screen of the sat nav . . . it shouldn't take long. Looks like we pass a bunch of fields, then some *more* fields, then an entrance to a riding stable. As soon as we see a railway station, we'll know to look out for the supermarket, which is just beyond it.

I'm in charge of a shopping list that Gill scribbled down for us. It includes marshmallows (Margot insisted!). We're going to go to the firepit after tea tonight and toast them!

"So, how about this, Wanda, eh?" says Lee. "Who'd

have guessed I'd be driving to the supermarket with my other, *younger* daughter today?!"

Obviously, since I came across that secret stash of photos on Saturday in the loft room, all I've thought about is Lee. What he was like, how I could find him, what I'd ask if I was lucky enough to get to meet him . . . Apart from all the other noise and chatter in my head, those three thoughts have gone round and round and ROUND like an endless loop in my brain.

And wow, I have been SO lucky that it only took a single day to find my real-life father and realise that Lee is just as lovely as I wanted him to be. And now it's Day Two, and we're in the car together – just us, finally – and I can ask him anything I want. Only my head is absolutely clouded with thick, dense fog. I can't think of ANYTHING to ask. All I can do is sit here, hunched up in the passenger seat and scratching at my itchy head.

"So I know it's a lot to cover – like twelve years! – but how about you tell me a bit more about yourself, Wanda?" Lee asks cheerfully.

I'm glad he's got his eyes on the road in front, and

isn't just staring at me, or he'd see me getting more frozen by the second with the pressure of it all.

The thing is, I told Lee and Gill and Margot and Charlie quite a LOT of my story this morning at breakfast, and on the car journey to Badgers Bottom too, before I crashed out. They know about me and Patti travelling around ever since Gran died. I listed a bunch of the countries and cities and towns and villages and farms and places that me and my mum have visited over the years. They know – like Mr Swanson said yesterday – that I didn't have a clue who my dad was till I was looking through Patti's rucksack on Saturday, after the fire.

I don't know what else to say . . .

I think Lee guesses from my silence that I'm a bit stuck, so he speaks again.

"Okay, how about *I* start. I'm a physiotherapist and I work at the local hospital in Dover. I met Gill through a dating app nearly . . . ten years ago, it must be? She does admin for a local firm, but works from home."

So it was Gill's office I slept in last night. I don't know what people who do admin *do* exactly, but it explains all the tech on the desk – a shiny Mac computer and a scanner and big printer. It was a LOT fancier than the ancient PC back in Hélène's office at the farm.

"And Gill already had Margot when we met, so we became an instant family!" Lee carries on. "Then Charlie came along, of course!"

At that point, there's a strange high-pitched squeak of a noise, and we both glance at each other.

"Hope the car's not thinking of packing up," says Lee, now frowning at the dashboard, in case any warning messages have flashed up. They haven't; phew. "I've lost my mobile, more or less, so we're in trouble if we break down!"

"I've got mine!" I say, taking my small not-a-smartphone out of the pocket of the hoodie Margot lent me.

"Look at that; Wanda to the rescue – again!" Lee laughs. "But let's not worry . . . can't hear anything now. So come on – *your* turn. If it makes it easier, just tell me three things about yourself."

In an instant, about eleventy-thousand-trillion things start floating around, just about visible, in my head-fog. And – doh! – I end up reaching for the most boring one.

"My favourite colour is blue," I say, then wince. My mind is now flooded with images of blue seas and skies and the blue of the tiny Greek flag on my teddy's little waistcoat.

"Mine too!" Lee agrees. "Okay, hit me with *another* Wanda fact."

More of the eleventy-thousand-*trillion* things swirl around again, and I pick one that makes me a bit sad this time.

"I miss my gran's hugs," I say. "She was really good at hugs."

"You know something?" says Lee. "I do remember Patti – your mum, I mean – talking about your gran. We both spoke about our families over that summer we were together . . . your gran sounded nice, but I think she worried about Patti being so young and travelling on her own. Patti got pretty annoyed by that!"

"Sounds like Gran – and Patti!" I say, feeling a tiny bit more comfortable, feeling my shoulders start to relax.

"Yeah, and I remember telling Patti about *my* mum, and how she was pretty crazy and sang all the time and was a lot of fun," Lee carries on. "Patti said she liked the sound of the amazing Wanda Swanson!"

"Was that why she named me after her?" I ask, suddenly flushing with pride at being named after someone so cool-sounding. The *amazing* Wanda Swanson!

"I guess it must've been," Lee says, nodding, as I sneak a sideways look at him.

Now that I'm feeling a bit less shy and stuck, I feel brave enough to ask Lee a question. A really touchy, hard question.

"So how come you didn't stay in touch with Patti?"

And find out about ME, I want to add, but don't.

"I wanted to stay in touch. I really, really did, Wanda. But the plan was that Patti would look me up when she got back to the UK, in a couple of months, after she finished travelling. She had my details. But I never heard from her," Lee says wistfully. "I just thought maybe she didn't like me as much as I liked her. *Loved* her, I mean."

Lee goes a bit quiet. I feel bad for asking that

question now. Especially since my history is old history, and he has his really nice family now, in the present.

"But hey, come on," he suddenly says brightly, "you still owe me one more fact, Wanda!"

So I'm back to the eleventy-thousand-trillion swirly thoughts in my head, and one pops right out at me and demands I say it out loud.

"I have ADHD."

"Really?" says Lee. "I wouldn't have guessed! I thought people with ADHD were more . . . I dunno . . . well, talked a lot, maybe?"

"I do sometimes talk a lot out loud," I tell him. "I mean, once you get to know me better, you'll see. But most of the time, there's just non-stop talking *inside my head*."

"Wow! So that's a symptom, is it? Well, I've learnt something today!" says Lee. "And, oh, I've thought of another one; what about impulsiveness? I thought that was an ADHD thing for sure. And you're not particularly impulsive, are you, Wanda? Oh, wait a minute . . .!"

We both exchange looks again. And burst out

laughing at the same time, as the thought of my mad stowaway adventure pops immediately into both our minds.

I'm laughing till the tears stream down my face.

I'm loving hearing the deep laugh of my actual dad.

But then I stop, because someone ELSE is laughing along.

There's a giggle coming from the back of the car, from the boot . . .

"Lee," I say quickly.

He's laughing so much and concentrating on the road, so he doesn't properly hear me at first.

"LEE!" I repeat louder. "There's someone in the car!"

"What?!" says Lee, quickly indicating and pulling over to the side of the country road.

He swivels his head around. We're both staring towards the rear of the estate car.

"BOO!" says Charlie, jumping up from the boot.

"Charlie!" Lee barks. "What on earth are you doing?"

"I stowed away! Just like Wanda!!" Charlie announces, scrabbling over the back seat and sliding into his booster, clicking a seatbelt over himself as if everything was fine and normal. "It was fun!"

"Well, that was actually a very silly and dangerous thing to do. And you mum is going to be SO worried about where you are. Can I borrow your mobile to call her, Wanda?"

I hand over my little phone, and he starts quickly inputting a number.

"Why did you call Dad 'LEE', Wanda?" Charlie asks me. "He's Dad! He's *your* dad! THAT'S what you're supposed to call him!"

Above the *brrr, brrr* of a distant ringing tone, Lee gazes over at me and grins.

"Charlie's been spectacularly wrong about a few things today," he says, "but I think he's right about this one, Wanda. Call me Dad, okay? Oh – hello? Gill? No, I know – don't worry, I've got him. He's with me. Me and Wanda . . ."

CALL ME DAD.

Charlie's made my heart nearly jump out of my chest twice today, but I am so grateful to him for helping make those three words happen.

Can this day get any more awesome?

MARGOT

Hey Diary,

It's nearly midnight, and the first day of the holiday has been really great!

Well, apart from Charlie giving Mum a couple of heart attacks, cos of the pond incident and stowing away on the shopping trip. He was pretty good the rest of the day. Sort of. The farmer did have to ask Charlie not to be so loud when he was feeding the goats, in case he scared them, but Charlie doesn't have an off-button sometimes, so he kept shouting the way he does and then one of the goats headbutted him in the bum and shoved him over. Served him right! But of course Charlie thought it was the best thing ever and probably hopes he'll get butted in the bum again tomorrow.

And it's been so nice hanging out with Wanda. Charlie just LOVES her, cos she's got lots of time for him and doesn't mind chattering a load of rubbish with him – unlike me! He's been following her around like he's her one-person Fan Club! It's pretty sweet. And then me and Wanda helped Dad chop the vegetables and we made tacos for tea together. We were going to go up to the firepit with the marshmallows after that, but a family from one of the other cottages was up there using the barbeque, so our toasting session will have to wait till tomorrow. BTW, Wanda's not so shy now; during dinner and after she talked more about all the places she's lived and about stuff her and her mum have done and seen. It was really fun to hear about. But wow, she talked so fast, we hardly managed to get a question in!

Anyway, I think Wanda's sleeping now, so I'll stop in a sec and turn the bedside light out. I'll just look at my phone or something. Just not at the socials where I might see Marisa's posts! I've promised myself I won't do that, or waste time thinking how good a time she's having without me . . .

Though speaking about people having a good time without me, I did feel a bit gutted earlier, when Esha and Sam came to our cottage in swimsuits and towels and asked if I wanted to come try out their hot tub, and maybe hang out at the barn later.

Mum jumped in and said thanks, but we were all having a special family night in tonight (cos of Wanda, she meant). The thing is, I really did want to hang out at the cottage – just all of us and Wanda – but I couldn't help feeling that little flutter, like I was missing out or something, I suppose? But there's always tomorrow night, right?

#FOMO

#TomorrowsAnotherDay

WANDA

I'm lying on my side, my head on the squashy pillow, watching my stepsister as she scribbles in her journal, leaning it up against her knees.

(What's she writing? Is it about ME? It has to be about me, doesn't it? And it has to be good because she's smiling. Yay!)

Between us is a table with a bedside lamp. The gentle light of it makes Margot's red hair shimmer, like it's on fire. It's beautiful.

Also on the small table are two precious things to me – my framed photo of Gran, and Teddy Theo, who's propped up against the white plastic frame. There's also a 'posey' of daisies in an egg cup right beside them – a gift left for me by Charlie, before he went to bed.

Charlie is SO adorable. When him and me and Dad were going around the supermarket earlier, I told him all about Babette and the other goats back at the farm, and then I taught him how to say 'goat' in Spanish, Croatian, Hindi, French and Arabic. Then when we all went to help the farmer at feeding time this afternoon, Charlie called out "CABRA!" and "JARAC!" and "BAKAREE!" and "CHÈVRE!" and "MAEAZA!", and I think the farmer was really impressed! But then one of the goats knocked Charlie over. Which was SO funny! I couldn't BREATHE I was laughing so much!

"Margot?" I say quietly, not wanting to disturb her while she's writing.

"Uh-huh?" says Margot, closing her journal with the pen inside, so it makes a bump.

She puts it under her pillow then lies down, facing me.

"I . . . I've had the best day," I tell her. "Like, the BEST, BEST, BEST day!"

And the absolute *best* of the BEST, BEST, BEST things is that I have a FAMILY and they really

LIKE me! They all listened to me when I was telling them stuff today, and they were interested in everything I had to say, and I found my voice and didn't feel shy any more!

"Me too," says Margot, giving me a softer-glow version of her sunshine smile. She reaches her hand out to me, and I take it, and I think my heart is going to KA-BOOM! with happiness.

BTW, I've told someone else tonight how happy I am. I told Patti! While Margot was in the bathroom brushing her teeth, I texted my mum. I told her that I was having the most amazing time without her, and she didn't need to bother coming for me at the weekend. (Okay, so *technically* I got as far as '. . . don't bother coming for me a—' and then my phone ran out of battery, and I remembered the charger was still stuck in the wall in the loft room back in France.)

Maybe I shouldn't have said all that, but I'm still angry with her and I don't care.

"And how about we have a BETTER-THAN-BEST day tomorrow?" says Margot.

"Yes, please!" I beam at her.

"See you in the morning," she says, gently letting go of my hand and reaching up to turn out the light. Just as she clicks the switch, she giggles and adds, "Goodnight, sis!"

"Night, sis!" I giggle too, at the newness and complete *wonderfulness* of that tiny, three-letter word.

Anyway, I'm so excited that I don't know how I'm supposed to get to sleep, but I'd better try, cos the sooner I sleep, the sooner it's tomorrow, when me and Margot and my brilliant family can begin our BETTER-THAN-BEST day!

TUESDAY

WANDA

I watched Margot sleeping for ages this morning, just hoping all the staring might wake her up. We had to get started on our next brilliant day!

By the way, there's *actually* a real, true, scientific fact that explains why a person can tell they're being stared at. It's not because they're spookily psychic or something, but because humans happen to have insanely good 'peripheral' (i.e. all around) vision from our *caveman* past, when our whole nervous system would've been hyper-alert for threats and danger, e.g. sabre-toothed tigers coming to snack on us. So, yeah, that's the science, but I still like that people call it 'spidey-sense', as if it's a superhero skill. That's funny.

Anyway, I tried staring Margot out of her teenage

lie-in, but it didn't work, cos her spidey-sense was switched off, what with her eyes being closed and her snoring a little bit and everything. Boo.

I gave up and got dressed instead, since I could hear Charlie singing 'Baby Shark'. The song (racket) was coming from the kitchen, so that's where I went, and that's where I came across Dad and Gill sitting at the table, looking tired and nursing mugs of coffee. They both winced when Charlie LAUNCHED himself at me with an ear-splitting whoop, wrapping his arms around my neck and his legs around my waist.

Once I got my breath back, Dad said he had a great idea; could I do him and Gill a favour and take Charlie on the morning feeding session with the farmer?

Of *course* I said yes.

Though it was a bit early for that at first, so me and Charlie passed the time by making a 'road' out of the entire contents of the cutlery drawer. We laid wooden spoons and plastic salad servers and shiny forks and knives and stuff in two long, parallel lines that wound all around the living-room furniture. Charlie had a toy Jeep with him that was too small for shark passengers but the perfect size for Teddy Theo, so we *brmm-brmm*-ed him all the way along the knife-fork-spoon freeway. Dad had laughed, saying it was a lot better than Charlie watching endless cartoons in the morning.

And then when we heard the clang of the bell in the yard to say it was feeding time for the animals, me and Charlie shot off.

Eventually, after all the food pellets were shared out, we were still having way too much fun to go back to the cottage, so we are now having an educational march around the farm. So far, the cows, goats, Loki the llama and Danny the donkey have all been very impressed by the vocabulary I've been teaching my half-brother.

"Helado de fresa!" I call out.

"Strawberry ice-cream!" Charlie responds.

"Helado de menta choc!"

"Mint chocolate ice-cream!"

"Helado de límon!"

"Lemon ice-cream! Yuck . . ."

"Helado de chicle!"

"TICKLE ice-cream!"

"No, silly!" I say, bending over to tickle Charlie's tummy.

"Noooo!! Stop it, Wanda! Ha! I mean BUBBLE-GUM ice-cream!" he giggles. "Oh, wow – look – how does it turn on?"

Charlie's suddenly picked up a garden hose that's lying curled at the side of the Games Room building. He's waving it around and already eyeing up the tap it's attached to.

"I'm pretending to be you, Wanda! Putting out a fire!" he yelps.

"Yep, let's not do that," I say, before he's tempted to soak Esha and Sam, who are stretched out nearby on the deckchairs by the pond, staring at us sort of *blankly* through their dark sunglasses. (I think Charlie and me just seem too much like noisy little kids to them.)

And uh-oh . . . my spidey-senses suddenly make me aware that we're being watched, and not just by a couple of chickens pecking around or by the disapproving twins.

We're also being watched by an older man who's standing near the outbuildings.

Mr Swanson raises his hand to greet us.

"POPS!!" shouts Charlie and shoots off from my side.

I follow Charlie, though I'm not sure if I'm intruding – there's a big grandad/grandkid hug going on right now. Also, I'm not sure if Mr Swanson's going to be too pleased to see me.

Unless he's here to take me to the authorities, I suddenly panic. Is Mr Swanson turning up here a bad omen or something?

"Hello, Wanda. Good to see you again," he says, reasonably cheerfully. But of course, that could be a cover!

"Why did you come, Pops? I thought you didn't want to!" Charlie demands.

"Oh, let's not worry about that . . . I'm here now. Don't want to miss out on all the fun with the family, do I?"

He turns and motions us to follow him back to Barn Owl Cottage.

Wait – will there be a social worker waiting inside for me?

Or a POLICE OFFICER?

I'm ready to pause by the door, and am all set to reverse, to turn and *run*, to who knows where . . .

But, hey, it's okay!

Inside the cottage there's just Gill and Dad and a bunch of flowers on the table that Mr Swanson must have brought. It looks like something someone would bring when they're trying to make up. Patti would do that with Gran, whenever they fell out.

But I can't help noticing that Gill has one of those smiles that seem empty. Like the smile hasn't quite reached up to her eyes. A smile mask. I recognise it because it's the sort of smile I've given Patti every time she says we're moving again.

Gill's not a hundred per cent happy to have Mr Swanson here, is she?

"So, I'll get settled in my shepherd's hut, and then I'll come back and we can make our plan for the day, yes?" says Mr Swanson. "There's that hill walk we can do. Amazing views from the top, I read in the guidebook that I—"

"Oh, but Dad," I interrupt, turning to Lee when I remember something important, "when me and Charlie saw the farmer just now, he said he might organise a llama trek this afternoon . . ."

"Yes! I REALLY, REALLY want to do the llama trek!"

Charlie yelps.

The fact that there's a llama trek that might clash with his hill-climbing plans doesn't seem to register with Mr Swanson. Something else has grabbed his attention. Something specific that I just happen to have said without thinking.

"She called you *'Dad'*?" repeats Mr Swanson, sounding confused, looking from me to his son.

"Well, of *course* she's going to call me 'Dad'. What else would Wanda call me?" says my lovely, wonderful, caring father.

"I don't know, but isn't it all a bit soon, Louis? I mean, technically, Wanda might be my only granddaughter—"

I hear the tiniest but sharpest of gasps from Gill.

"—but I don't think she and I are quite ready to be so familiar with each other."

Gill's gasp doesn't seem to have registered with Mr Swanson. He's now too busy getting something out of a bag. It's a laptop.

"Actually, Wanda, I did some research when I was at home yesterday and found something we can take a look at together," he says, opening up the computer.

"When you first came to my house, I think you or your friend Elf mentioned that it had taken around two hours to drive from the farm in France to the ferry, right? So I searched for the term 'eco-farm' and found several in a large radius that might cover where you've been living. We can go through the names of these places and see if any of them ring any bells . . ."

I feel sick. It really IS a bad omen having Mr Swanson come. He really is determined to spoil everything. Yesterday I felt sorry for him, thinking maybe he felt a bit lonely and didn't have control of stuff any more. But I certainly don't want him to feel better by having control over ME!

"Hey!" says Dad, spotting my face fall and gently closing the top of Mr Swanson's computer. "Let's leave this till later, eh?

Mr Swanson looks like he's about to protest but is suddenly distracted by a very loud yawn.

"Hey, Pops . . ." mumbles Margot, finally awake and leaning in the living-room doorway. She's scratching sleepily at her head. "What are you doing here?"

"Just come to see you lovely lot, of course, Margot!" says Mr Swanson, holding his arms out for her to come in for a hug, same as Charlie a couple of minutes ago.

I don't suppose I'll ever be included in a grandkid hug . . . but then I don't think I really want to be.

"What made you change your mind and come?" Margot mutters, pretty quickly dipping in and then exiting the hug, scratching at her head again, this time more irritably.

But as she steps back, I see Margot stumble and wince, as her bare foot meets an unexpected spoon.

"Whoah!" says Mr Swanson, steadying her. "What is this mess?"

He looks down at the wending cutlery freeway me and Charlie made this morning.

"It's a road!" says Charlie.

"It's a hazard, is what it is. Time to tidy it up, Charlie," says Mr Swanson matter-of-factly. "Come on!"

"I'll help" I say.

"No, Wanda – Charlie's a big boy, and he can do it himself," says Mr Swanson. "Can't you, Charlie?"

Charlie looks up at his Pops and then flops down to a kneel on the carpet, picking up a single yellow picnic fork. He looks off at the rest of our 'road', and

I can see that he doesn't know where to start with all the cutlery trails winding off. Where the big wooden spoons go compared to the normal metal ones. If the plastic picnic stuff goes with them or in a different container. And what about random stuff like the salad servers and the chopstick set we'd come across. The thought of trying to sort it all out by himself is too overwhelming, I can tell. His eyes are filling with I-don't-know-how-to-do-this tears.

"Oh, for goodness' sake, it's only some silly cutlery," says Mr Swanson. "I really can't see what the problem is! You're not a lazy boy, are you, Charlie?"

I think Mr Swanson thinks the 'lazy' comment is somehow helpful, but of course it's not. It's the opposite.

Back when I was in Mrs Chopra's class, there was a supply teacher one day when Mrs Chopra was off sick. The supply said the same thing to me, when I accidentally spilled glitter on the floor during an art lesson. He asked if I was lazy when I didn't wipe the mess up from the floor straightaway. What he couldn't see was that my mind was in hyper-drive, flipping back and forth between two options . . .

1) Wet paper towels: would they make the glitter's colour leak and stain the floor tiles?
2) A vacuum from the cleaners' cupboard: this might be better, but would clumps of the glittery bits clog up the mechanism?

So I wasn't being lazy at all; I was trying to work out the best (or least worst) solution, and it was taking a while because of all the whirly hamster wheels. It was taking a while because I had ADHD!

Suddenly I feel a wave of heat in my face, *maddened* at the memory of the supply teacher who made me feel so bad about myself.

"Leave him alone!" I find myself snapping at Mr Swanson. "Charlie's not lazy – he has ADHD, same as me!"

I hear another little gasp coming from the direction of Gill. I look around at her and she looks even more tired and upset. Wait, did *I* do that? But I'm trying to help!

"I think you're very much wrong there, Wanda, dear," says Mr Swanson, making the 'dear' sound like something fed-up and grumpy, not friendly like it's supposed to be. "Charlie's just a typical, boisterous little boy. He just needs some clear boundaries."

Gill storms out of the room at that point.

"Dad . . .!" says my dad.

"What?" says Mr Swanson, defensively. "What have I said now?"

And then, unable to stop himself, Mr Swanson reaches down to stop Charlie scratching his head.

"What's going on with you two?" he says, nodding down at Charlie and then over to Margot, who's scratching again at her *own* head. "You're acting as if you both have nits!"

"That's probably because *I've* got nits and they've caught them from me!" I blurt out.

ADHD can also be like a truth drug. I can't pretend I don't have the answer to something when I absolutely do.

But when I look around at everyone's faces, it's like I've admitted I have the *plague*.

It's definitely not looking like it's going to be my BETTER-THAN-BEST day after all . . .

MARGOT

OMG, Diary,

I've got nits! Wanda gave us all NITS!

And because Mum got a migraine and had to lie down, Dad decided that we'd all go in the car – him, me, Wanda, Charlie and Pops – and pick up some nit shampoo (family pack!) from the pharmacy in the town nearby. Fun holiday activity! NOT!!

And as if that wasn't mortifying enough, Dad went on to sledgehammer us with the news that as we were close to the hill Pops had seen in the guidebook, we might as well walk up it on the way back from buying the nit shampoo. Got to keep Pops happy, right?!

So we all climbed a hill I didn't want to climb, saw a view I didn't care about, all while Charlie whined about missing the chance to hang out with Lenny the llama and Wanda stayed silent.

And what I couldn't say to anyone – cos it would've made everything a thousand times worse – was that I'd heard what Pops had said this morning.

I heard it as I stood outside the living room. Pops didn't seem that keen on Wanda, but the funny thing (and when I say 'funny' thing, I clearly mean pretty awful thing) is that it seems he still prefers to think of Wanda as his 'real' granddaughter, rather than me, who he's known all these years.

Honestly, all I want to do right now is go home. Either that, or go and hang out with Esha and Sam, who don't know anything about my stupid, dysfunctional family.

But first, I have to put up with Mum tugging and combing this horribly chemical-smelling nit-killing stuff through my hair in a minute.

I'd better go get it over with . . .

#SmellsSoGross

#Urgh

#NitsAreEvil

WANDA

Everyone is somewhere, but no one is together.

Mr Swanson went straight to his shepherd's hut after the no-fun hill-walk.

Dad is outside, on his phone – I heard him leaving a message for Patti (again) when he walked past the French doors of mine and Margot's bedroom a minute ago. He can't wait to get rid of me.

As for Margot, she's in the shower, washing off the nit treatment.

Charlie is watching 'Shark Tale' in the living room, while *his* nit treatment is still on and doing its stuff.

Gill is in the kitchen, with her plastic gloves on, waiting for me and nit treatment number three, I guess. I'm just too scared to go through there until she calls me. I've done everything wrong and made everyone miserable today, because I'm completely useless.

If I wasn't here they'd all be happier.

Like Patti; *she'd* be happier without me trailing behind her on her travels, spoiling all her fun.

I spoiled Elif's fun too, making her worried about getting into trouble with the police or Customs. Making her late for meeting up with her cousins.

I spoil EVERYONE'S fun.

What's even the POINT of me?

"Wanda . . . ready?" says Gill, sticking her head around the bedroom door. She has dark circles under her eyes. *I* caused them.

"Mm-hmm," I mumble, getting up and following her though to the kitchen.

She gestures to a chair, and I sit down on it.

"Right, let's do this," I hear her say, as she wraps a black plastic bin-bag around my shoulders and fastens it with a clothes-peg.

I'm glad she's standing behind me. I don't want to see the disappointment in her face.

"I'm sorry I gave Margot and Charlie nits and messed

up everyone's day . . ." I whisper my feeble apology.

"Don't worry about the nits, Wanda," I hear Gill say. "It's just one of those things. There's just a lot going on at the moment . . ."

I don't know what 'a lot' is, but I bet most of it is MY fault. I start sinking into a pit of gloom when a sharp, bitter stench jolts me back out of it.

"Urgh!!" I say wincing. "That is GROSS!"

"Nit shampoo?" says Gill, with just the hint of a wry smile in her voice. "Well, yes! It smells revolting! Have you never had a treatment for it before?"

"No!' I say, pinching my nose and coughing a little bit.

"You've never had nits?" she asks, sounding surprised now.

"Yes – LOTS of times!" I say. "But Patti doesn't believe in chemicals . . ."

"I see," says Gill, carrying on dib-dabbing at my head with stinky VILENESS.

I don't know what she meant by 'I see'. It sounds kind of *judgey*.

"Listen, I'm sure your mum really cares about you and loves you . . ."

It sounds like Gill wants to add, 'in her own way'.

". . . in her own way," she adds, right on cue.

That's a bit judgey-sounding again. I don't really like anyone being judgey about Patti except me. That's MY job.

"But I just wondered, is there anything else your mum doesn't . . . you know . . . believe in?"

Gill's trying to get at something, but I'm not sure what. She sounds kind of awkward . . .

I suddenly blush. She's not talking about periods, is she?! But then that doesn't make sense; why would Patti 'not believe' in periods? So it can't be that. But then what is it? The trouble is, I can't think properly because my entire nervous system is screaming HORRIBLE SMELL!! SENSORY-OVERLOAD ALERT!!

I end up saying something, *anything*, just so there's not an uncomfortable silence between us.

"She doesn't believe in labels."

"Labels?" says Gill, sounding confused.

"Like names . . . 'Mum', 'Dad', that sort of thing," I explain. "It's why I call her Patti. And she doesn't believe in labels for people like . . . having ADHD."

There. I've said it. Again. But then I can't make

things any worse, can I? (Yeah, probably . . .)

"Well, Patti might not believe in it, but she still got you a diagnosis, right?" says Gill. I can't tell from the tone in her voice if she's mad at me for mentioning it.

"No, she didn't. It was my primary school teacher who suggested it," I tell her. "Mrs Chopra thought it might be why I did certain things, like just zoning out in her lessons. Or Mrs Chopra would be telling us step-by-step instructions for what she needed us to do in our workbooks, and everyone else understood straight away, but with me she'd have to go over the instructions heaps of times."

"Okay," I hear Gill say.

It's true. I'd listen to Mrs Chopra's first instruction and totally get it, then during the second one, I'd be repeating the first one in my head to be sure I really DID get it, then by the third, I'd be thinking, 'Hey, what happened to the second point?', and by the fourth one I was wondering what Mrs Chopra's first name was and I bet it was something pretty and then realise a couple of the other kids were pointing at me and laughing.

"Look, I'm sorry I said that stuff this morning . . ."

177

I tell Gill. "About Charlie. Maybe he doesn't have ADHD."

I'm pretty sure my brother has ADHD.

I just don't want Gill hating me.

Gill doesn't say anything for a second, which makes me think she still hates me.

"It's just quite difficult, Wanda," Gill says finally, as the cold of the stinky nit treatment now feels as if it's soaking in all over my head. "Charlie's gorgeous, but he's quite hard work. And Paul – your grandfather – has very specific ideas about how we should be dealing with his behaviour."

No wonder Gill hates me, if I'm making things even MORE complicated for her than they already are.

"Anyway, right – you're done," she announces. "Leave this on for twenty minutes then wash it off in the shower. Okay?"

Actually, yes, I AM suddenly okay!

Cos I've JUST had an idea of how I can at least TRY to make things better. I'm very scared by my idea, but whatever, I'm going to do it!

"Thanks," I say, getting up off the chair. I'm about to leave the kitchen and go do The Big Scary Thing, but Gill rests her hand on my arm.

"Wanda . . . is there anything else? Anything else your mum doesn't, y'know, believe in? That maybe I could help you with?"

My head starts whirling, trying to figure out what Gill's going on about. Patti doesn't believe in a whole *bunch* of stuff, like preservatives and washing your hair too often (affects the oils in it) and wearing non-natural fabrics and burning fossil fuels and using pesticides (BOO!) and putting pineapple on pizza and Western ideals of education and some evil sweetener in soft drinks that I can't remember the name of and Christmas cards cos they're a waste of trees, and a whole lot more. But I can't see how Gill knowing that stuff would do any good and I don't know why she thinks I need help with any of it?

"I . . . er . . . don't think so," I say vaguely.

I hurry back to the bedroom, expecting to see Margot, but the French doors are open and she's gone off somewhere. That's okay because I've got to go somewhere too. I head over the courtyard in the direction of the field.

My head stinks, and the plastic binbag fastened

round my shoulders is flip-flapping like a 99p store Batman cape as a walk, but that's okay. What's not so okay is that over to the right, by the duckpond, I can see Margot sitting with Esha and Sam, all smiley on the deckchairs there. They look chatty and comfy and grown-up. Margot is actually laughing, which she hasn't done all day (my fault again).

But I can't think too much about that; I have The Big Scary Thing to do. So I keep flip-flapping as fast as I can, into the field with the funny-looking shepherd's hut things in them. I know which one is Mr Swanson's because I can see him now, sitting outside it on a camping chair, looking at his computer. I bet he's busy researching meditation retreats within a hundred-mile radius of every eco-farm in France . . .

As I come closer to him, he closes his computer and stares at me, wondering why a twelve-year-old girl he barely knows is stomping over to him with a scowl on her face, hair that's slimy and toxic-smelling and wearing a very basic, homemade superhero costume.

"Wanda?" he says, in a questioning sort of a way.

Here we go. I am about to do The Big Scary Thing.

Or I *could* turn around and not bother.

I feel really sick.

JUST DO IT, WANDA!!

Yes.

Okay.

Deep breath.

I'm going to start . . .

"When I was in primary school, a whole bunch of kids in my class said I was stupid. But I wasn't; I always got good marks in the end," I babble in Mr Swanson's direction. "I just needed things explained a bit more at first, cos my brain wouldn't stop drifting off, and wondering why the cloud outside the window looked like a carrot and why some bees were skinny and looked more like wasps and how come honey bees didn't overheat in the summer since they were so fluffy and why picture books for little kids all made out that pirates were super fun when they were actually really, really horrible people."

I stop for a quick breath. Mr Swanson looks as if he's about to talk so I dive back in before he gets the chance.

"The thing is, my brain is like a bunch of hamster

wheels that are going at a million miles an hour and sometimes I can't stop thinking and thinking and thinking and worrying and then – BOOM! – I'm just so tired that I want to lie down for ages and my entire body feels like it's made of sludge."

"Listen, Wanda, dear," says Ms Swanson, "I've been Googling and—"

Nope. I'm going to interrupt him because a) that's what people with ADHD are pretty good at, and b) if I don't I'll lose my place and forget what I'm saying, and THAT'S why people with ADHD interrupt a lot.

"So I do think that Charlie might have ADHD, even if YOU don't, cos it can run in families and I'm his half-sister and, yeah, so we're not exactly the same, cos ADHD is different for everyone, but I can see stuff in him that I recognise. And you know, it's all right if he DOES have ADHD, because ADHD just means your brain handles things or struggles with things in different ways. It's like if you are left-handed and everything in the world is made for right-handed people cos there are more of them. And it's okay, cos if you're left-handed, you can still

DO everything but it's just a bit harder and you have to concentrate more, which is tiring. Obviously."

"Fine, but if I could just say—"

"*Also,*" I interrupt again, because I have to get all this out of my head, "you probably don't know but LOADS of really successful and creative and famous people have ADHD and loads of ordinary people have it too and they have jobs they're great at and it's fine. Charlie is fine. Charlie is ace!"

My heart is pumping like I've run a marathon. I haven't any words left. Mr Swanson can say what he likes now, but I have done The Big Scary Thing (i.e. rant at a quite old grown-up) and that's the best I can do. The best I can do for my lovely little half-brother.

Except maybe there is another Big Scary Thing I can do, this time for my stepsister . . .

"And then this morning you called me your 'only' granddaughter, and for a start, you don't act like I am your grandkid and also that is REALLY bad, because if Margot heard that, she would be SO upset, and I think it makes Gill really sad."

"What? That's ridiculous!" Mr Swanson blusters, using his favourite word. "I mean, yes, well of *course*

Margot is my grandchild. In a way. I mean, not *biologically* but—"

"What's the difference, Mr Swanson, hmm?!" I butt in.

I feel instant BLAZING with the injustice of him gibbering on about 'biology', when all a family means is caring about each other. Not looking for 'differences'. I mean, who cares about 'halfs' and 'steps' in term of family. Isn't that just—

"Why are you calling him Mr Swanson?" comes a voice from inside the shepherd's hut. "That's so silly! His name's Pops – you HAVE to call him Pops, Wanda!"

Charlie comes and stands at the door of the pod. His hair is all greasy and messy with nit treatment and he has smudges of coloured pen on his face. I guess he must've got bored watching 'Shark Tale' and come up to hang out with his grandfather.

"I don't think he wants me to call him that," I tell Charlie, tilting my chin up defiantly.

"No I didn't say *that*, exactly!" Mr Swanson protests. "It's just that—"

"Course he does!" Charlie cheerfully talks over his grandfather, while stepping out of the shepherd's hut and holding something out to me. "Anyway, I did something for you, Wanda. I know you like rainbows because they're on your bag!"

Charlie hands me Teddy Theo.

But Teddy Theo is not quite looking himself.

"Oh dear, Charlie," mutters Mr Swanson. "I thought you were just doing some colouring in, on paper, I mean!"

My little brother must've concentrated *really* hard on drawing the red and yellow and green and orange felt-pen lines that are so neatly arc-ed across Teddy Theo's worn-but-fluffy face.

"*NOOOOOOOOOOOOOO!*" I shout, feeling like my little slice of childhood has been ripped away from me, and not caring in that second that Charlie's lip is wobbling and he's started crying.

Ha! I thought today was going to be my BETTER-THAN-BEST day and it turns out that I got that so wrong it hurts.

Today sucks.

SUCKS.

MARGOT

Hey Diary,

Just a quiet teatime moan, since I've got the room to myself. (Wanda's been in the bath for about an hour.)

What a weird day. I mean, not just weird, but kind of terrible? Everyone seemed to be in such bad moods. Including me, I guess.

But there was one good bit . . . after my shower and washing off the nit treatment earlier, I was feeling all 'arrrghhh!', so I just took myself off for a walk, and ended up seeing Esha and Sam waving at me from the seats around the duck pond. It was great to flop down beside them and just be like a teenager, knowing we all fitted together! (How jealous would Marisa be, if she could see me hanging out with two super-cool sixteen-year-old girls, when she thinks I'm such a baby.)

You know, hanging out with Esha and Sam, maybe it felt so good because I just needed a break from the whole family. Yeah, even Wanda. (Sorry, Wanda.) It's all just too intense . . .

Anyway, the twins were asking me how my day had gone and then I rolled my eyes and told them all about Wanda's surprise gift of nits and they were "ewwing!!" and laughing and that got me laughing which felt so good after a disaster of a day.

I did feel kind of mean when they pointed out Wanda flapping her way across the courtyard with that binbag around her shoulders, but whatever. Shoudn't say this, but she did look so lame! And then without going into it, I told them she wasn't my actual sister; just a stepsister, and Esha said, "Ah, well that makes sense!" and I wasn't sure why it made sense but it sort of helped make me feel less responsible for Wanda and less embarrassed by her.

Okay, I'd better stop – Dad's calling for me. We're going to have a barbeque at the firepit tonight, which should be pretty awful, since I think everyone's kind of angry or hurt or offended by everyone else . . .

#MoreLater

PS. This would make Marisa jealous too; it's the twins' last night here at the farm – they're going home in the morning – but me and Esha and Sam have swapped numbers and everything!

WANDA

The blue of the sky has that mush of yellow, peach and orange in it that means the sun is thinking about setting soon.

And – SLAP! – little bitey bugs are giving my ankles one last nibble or two before their bedtime, as me and Dad and everyone sit on the logs around the firepit.

The smell of our barbeque still hangs in the air, and specks of breadcrumbs from the burger buns are scattered on the ground, where the chickens will have fun finding them in the morning.

Things have been a bit better tonight. Dad and Gill and Wanda and Mr Swanson have been quite nice and polite to each other and to me.

Maybe someone else – someone who's not paranoid like I am – would think everything was okay again. They'd think the grumbly, gritty, uncomfortable bits of the day had just rubbed away. But I don't know if that's true . . . it's like everyone's being TOO polite. The conversations have been TOO nicey-nice and boring. ("Mmm, this salad's good!"; "Is the bed in the shepherd's hut comfortable enough for you, Paul?"; "The ducklings are so sweet, aren't they?"; "Which are your favourite animals on the farm, Charlie?")

It all feels fake. It's like there's another, unknown, secret conversation going on underneath, and it's bound to be about ME, isn't it?

And as for Margot – last night, we were getting close like sisters, and tonight she's sort of acting as if she's a smiley stranger . . .

Actually, there is one person who's their normal self. Charlie is just being Charlie, which at this moment involves kicking a ball he's found against the outside wall of the Games Room . . .

THUD-*UNK*, THUD-*UNK*, THUD-*UNK* . . .

I mean, I'm still feeling bruisey and sad about

what happened to Teddy Theo, but me and Charlie have made up. Before we came here to the firepit, I'd found him sitting crosslegged on my bed, with a note for me and a biscuit. The note said 'SORY WNADA I LOV YO' in all the different pen colours he'd used to deface my teddy, and the biscuit was only half a biscuit cos apparently I took a very long time in the bath and he got hungry waiting.

THUD-*UNK*, THUD-*UNK*, THUD-*UNK* . . .

"Better think about getting Charlie to bed soon," murmurs Gill, as she gathers up our paper plates. "He's going to be driving everyone in the other cottages mad with that ball!"

"We've still got to toast our marshmallows, though, don't we?" Margot reminds everyone, holding up the wooden skewers Dad bought specially in the supermarket yesterday.

"Actually, I think I'll have an early night myself," says Mr Swanson. He's sitting next to me, and leans over to say quietly, "And maybe we can have a little catch-up in the morning, Wanda? After breakfast?"

Help! I don't want to have a little catch-up with Mr Swanson! He probably wants to tell me he's zoomed in on a Google Earth image and spotted me feeding Babette or something.

But before I can think of a suitable answer for him, Dad calls over to me.

"Chuck me the bag of marshmallows, Wanda!" he says, from the other side of the firepit. "They're just by your side . . ."

I reach down and grab a huge rustling bag of pink and white squooshiness.

"Here!" I say and throw it.

But a bitey bug chooses *that* particular second to nip me HARD on my ankle, and without thinking I reach down to whack the minibeast away.

So at same time as I give my ankle a sharp SLAP!, the bag I'm throwing changes trajectory, and instead of it sailing over towards Dad's waiting hands, I've slam-dunked it STRAIGHT into what's left of the fire.

Instant twists of bright flame dance up, as the plastic melts and fizzles and the sugar-fuelled marshmallows burn and turn to gloop.

There's a muddle of gasps and "oh, no!"s, though there's no danger (the flames are dialling down already), just a whole lot of disappointment.

"I'm sorry!" I begin yet ANOTHER apology. "I didn't mean to—"

My words are drowned out by a blast of water from a hose landing smack in the middle of the firepit, instantly extinguishing the sticky embers. At the same time, the watery jet forces hot ash upwards into a dramatic cascade that makes us all jump away from the pit.

"Charlie!" snaps Margot, snatching the hose from her brother and pointing it into the grass, where the water gurgles into the turf. "What did you do that for?"

"I put the fire out!" Charlie says. "Like Wanda did in France!"

The hosepipe snakes all the way back the tap against the side of the Games Room, where Charlie had been THUD-*UNK*, THUD-*UNK*, THUD-*UNK*-ing his ball just now. Dad's already following the trail back and is turning off the tap.

"Oh, Charlie . . ." Gill sighs, putting her head in her hands.

Charlie's grin of pride is quickly turning into a wobbly-bottomed lip of worry.

"Now, now," says Mr Swanson. "Give Charlie his

due – he was trying to do the right and safe thing and put out a fire."

"While trying to burn us all with hot ash!" Margot points out, brushing dark greys specks from her T-shirt and jeans, which only makes them smear more. "I feel like I'm in Pompeii . . ."

Right that second, I feel as melted and gloopy and *useless* as the dissolved marshmallows.

MARGOT

Hey Diary,

Wanda's asleep already. So's Charlie . . . he snuck into our bedroom a while ago with his pet shark and is curled up snoozing at the bottom of Wanda's bed, like a puppy.

I told Mum and Dad, but they said just to leave him there if he was comfy enough, and they'd take him through to the sofa bed in their room later, when the movie they were watching finished.

They've just put the movie on. I looked it up on my phone; it lasts for nearly two hours, which gives me LOTS of time! I've put a blankie over Charlie to keep him comfy, and I'm going to sneak out now . . .

#MyLittleSecret
#DontTell
#LipsSealed

WANDA

After we got back from the firepit, Gill suggested we all play a game of Junior Scrabble to help Charlie cheer up and wind down, but Charlie couldn't concentrate (neither could I) and got teary and grizzly (I felt the same).

Then Dad took Charlie off to bed to read him a story, so I just took myself off to bed too, leaving Margot in the living room with her mum.

I couldn't get to sleep, though; the cloud duvet and squashy pillows didn't feel right any more. It was as if their combined floofiness was trying to suffocate me. I hugged Teddy Theo with my eyes closed so I didn't have to see his punk'd face, and surprise, surprise, eventually I must've fallen asleep.

Cos now I've just woken up to several things that

are kind of surprising. The sky's a deep inky-black outside, with stars glittering. I can see this clearly because – surprise! – the French doors are open. I glance over at Margot's bed, but she's not in it.

Someone extra is in MY bed, though. Charlie's curled up at my feet. He's wearing a onesie and hugging his shark Eddy, with a blankie half on him.

I feel a huge rush of fondness for my kid brother, and don't disturb him as I get up to close the French doors.

But then I wonder if I *should* close them . . . where IS Margot? I don't want to stop her from getting back in, if she's just gone outside for some fresh air. Which doesn't actually *seem* like the sort of thing Margot would do at – I quickly check the digital clock on the chest of drawers – nearly eleven?

An itch of a thought suddenly squiggles in my head.

It's something I really shouldn't do.

But what if it helps me know where Margot is right now?

I bet Mr Swanson would say that's more-or-less a safeguarding issue, wouldn't he?

I bend down and slip my hand under Margot's

pillow. There's a soft light on the wall outside, one that'll help me see what she's written, so I stand at the open French doors, flip to today's entry in Margot's diary and read . . .

'I just needed a break from the whole family. Yeah, even Wanda. (Sorry, Wanda.) It's all just too intense . . .

'I did feel kind of mean when they pointed out Wanda flapping her way across the courtyard with that binbag around her shoulders, but whatever. Shouldn't say this, but she did look so lame!

'I said she wasn't my actual sister, just a stepsister, and Esha said, "Ah, well that makes sense!" and I wasn't sure why it made sense but it sort of helped make me feel less responsible for Wanda and less embarrassed by her.'

There's one more entry after that, talking about sneaking out tonight, talking about a secret she has.

But I'm too crushed to care about Margot's 'secrets' after seeing what she really thinks of me!

Only I hadn't realised that EVERYONE was suddenly being honest about their feelings . . . I can suddenly make out Dad and Gill talking, and I just heard my name being mentioned.

Tossing Margot's diary back on her bed, I step out into the warm night air and see that the matching set of doors to the living room are open, and the conversation inside is drifting out. I tiptoe along the cool grass lawn and listen . . .

"It's just all so hard, Louis!" Gill is saying. "I mean, Charlie is off the scale as it is. You *know* his teacher's always asking me in to talk about what he's up to. And then your dad wades in with unhelpful comments; then Wanda with all the ADHD talk. And now Charlie's so impressed with Wanda that he's started copying *everything* she's done, and nearly got himself drowned in the pond, and stowed away in the back of the car with no seatbelt and tonight with the fire and everything . . . Honestly, Louis – what's Charlie going to try to do next?"

I lean back against the cool stone wall.

So it's true; never mind The Big Scary Thing I tried to do today (speaking to Mr Swanson, I mean). I'm STILL making everything more complicated and difficult for my dad and his family.

I bet they wish I'd never turned up. I bet they wish—

The glint of light catches my eye.

It's coming from the Games Room building.

Is *that* where Margot is?

I don't know what I want to do. Confront her? Tell her how bad, how *sad* she's made me? Without a plan in my fizzy head, I start walking towards the building and the light, wincing as my bare feet leave the warmth of the grass and pad onto the cool, rounded cobbles of the yard. Around me, more soft light spills cosily from the blue-rimmed windows of the other cottages, families cuddled up and happy inside.

And now I'm by the field and by the wooden signpost. All the shepherd's huts are dark, except for Mr Swanson's (he's probably hunched over his laptop, hunting down my mum right this second). I take a right along the path and see the moonlight ripple across the deserted duckpond.

I'd normally expect the hamster wheels to start up about now, trying to randomly figure out unimportant things, like where the duck family have gone, and if they're as cuddled up and happy as the human guests in their converted farm buildings, or if Mama Duck has to keep a little, feathery radar tuned for danger at all times through the night.

But the hamster wheels don't work like that. Right now, all my energy is focused on my own internal radar.

Because my spidey-sense is telling me something doesn't feel quite right . . .

MARGOT

Dear Diary,

I'm in the Games Room. I'm writing this into Notes on my phone, cos my head wants to get all my thoughts down before they – pppfffffff! – flutter away! Ha! (I'll copy all this into your ACTUAL pages later – pinkie promise! If I remember . . .)

Anyway, the thing is, I don't want to be like stupid, annoying Marisa and take a bunch of stupid, show-off photos of what she's up to and stick it on stupid socials for everyone to gawp at. I just knew tonight would be special and different, hanging out here with Esha and Sam. So here I am, just snuggled on one of the sofas and typing it all down.

Guess what . . . Esha and Sam snuck some beers out of the fridge in their cottage and we've all had some! E & S said they drink with their friends ALL the time, and I pretended me and Marisa did too, but that's not true. The beer tasted totally, totally disgusting, but I feel kind of woozy, which's helped me forget how rubbish today was. (Is 'which's' a word? Like genuinely?)

Anyway, me and Esha and Sam had the best talks and ate all the crisps they brought. And we have been listening to music on the Bluetooth speak Sam has and then Esha lit this candle-in-a-jar she took from their cottage too and it smells amazing. It's sandalwood, Sam said, but I don't really know what sandalwood is except it is lush.

The thing is, I don't think Esha and Sam really do drink all the time with their mates because Sam is sort of sleeping (passed out?) on the other sofa and Esha is dancing around the little table in the middle where the candle is and she's looking like one of those wibbly-wobbly air-filled tube figures – HA! HA! – and she's spinning and laughing and she's a bit too wobbly and—

WANDA

I see the flames dance up practically the instant the candle goes flying, the dangerous brightness of it spilling out across the old rug on the barn floor.

WHOOSH . . .

"Just get out of there!" I yell from the doorway of the Games Room.

'Don't ever go in a burning building. Just get out and call the fire brigade.'

I know the rules. But Esha is screaming and jumping up and down and can't hear me. Margot locks eyes with me though – but her gaze is this weird mix of hazy and panicked.

"Come on!" I say, waving my hand at her.

Margot will have a mobile on her. Unlike me with my not-a-smartphone that's out of charge, all *regular* young people in the real world have theirs with them at all times. She can call 999, straight away. The town is really close. If it's got a train station and a big supermarket, it's *bound* to have a fire station.

"Sam! Sam's here!!" I see Margot mouth, above the hiss of the fire. She's leaning over one of the sofas.

Uh-oh. I hate breaking rules. I especially hate breaking rules if it involves fire licking its way across rugs and old bare, dry wooden floorboards and skedaddling up walls for fun, curling around dartboards, even.

But Esha's twin isn't getting up.

Without thinking it through – and feeling like I have no choice – I run inside, dive over to the sofa, where Margot is struggling to pull Sam up to a sitting position. With one of us on each side of her, Margot and me both hook our arms around the semi-conscious Sam and manage to hoist her up and off the sofa. She feels so heavy and hard to move, though.

"Quick! Help!!" I shout, and the unexpected fact that I'm even there seem to jolt Esha out of her panicked scream-state and she's suddenly scooping up her sister's legs and taking her weight as the three of us stumble together towards the double doorway where we can get out into the safety of the cool night air and—

A tremendous BLAST of cold water hits us all head on, chest on, and I'm struggling to breathe for water in my mouth, to keep my balance as the force batters into me. Same goes for Margot and Esha. Esha's let go her twin's legs and is suddenly knocked down and flailing on the floor. It's like the weight of the water is forcing us all back inside.

"No, no! Here! Give me that!" I make out a man's voice saying.

The jet of water now arcs over our heads. It must hit some of the fire because I can hear the hiss as the flames angrily let out their disappointment at being destroyed.

And now the four of us are like a jumble of arms and legs as we all get up and move forward again, getting ourselves out, out, out. Stumbling on all fours onto the cool, safe grass. Turning and looking up to see Mr Swanson, his jaw tight as he aims the jet from the hosepipe into the barn.

"It was me!" says a small voice, and I see Charlie jumping up and down on the spot. "I woke up and followed you, Wanda. And when I saw the fire, I shouted for Pops to come cos he was closest and I ran for the hosepipe, cos I know how to use it!!"

"Okay," I say breathlessly.

"Did I do good?" Charlie asks.

"Yeah, kind of," I mumble, realising he'd nearly knocked us all back inside.

I look at the others lying panting and shocked beside me; Margot and the twins.

And now concerned holidaymakers come streaming out of their duck-egg blue doors, in their PJs and hastily grabbed dressing gowns.

I'm instantly, overwhelmingly aware of SO many sounds.

The crackle and hiss as the fire tries to fight back.

The whoosh of water as Mr Swanson holds the hose in one hand, his mobile in the other, booming the name of the farm at some probably confused emergency services operator. "No . . . it's Badgers Bottom. Yes, I said *Bottom*!!"

It would be funny if the blood wasn't pumping

in my ears like I've got my head taped between two grandfather clocks.

And now I can hear a woman screaming, "Esha! Samira! My babies!!"

Two more names are being shouted. "Margot! Charlie!!"

Margot. Charlie.

No one's shouting, "Wanda!"

No one's shouting for me.

Why should they?

I flop back onto the carpet of dark grass and stare up at the stars.

Can I just be beamed up there, to the calm and the quiet, pretty please?

MARGOT

Diary,

I'm on my phone, on Notes, in an ambulance. AN AMBULANCE!

It's parked in the main courtyard, beside the fire engine. Sam left for hospital in another ambulance, to check she didn't inhale too much smoke. Esha followed with her parents, in their car. Mum told me this just now, before she left to check on Charlie. I mean, he's with Dad, but I guess Mum's still freaked at the idea of Charlie wandering out of the cottage all alone, late at night, and I've got to take the blame for that. But technically, Wanda should take the blame, shouldn't she? Since Charlie woke up and followed her out of the French doors . . .?

The paramedic here in the ambulance is worried I might have inhaled smoke as well and is making me wear an oxygen mask. There's a clip on my finger that's measuring . . . oh, I don't know what it's measuring!

But whatever, I don't need oxygen and measuring and the paramedic being nice to me. I don't deserve it!

I'll never hear from Esha and Sam after this, will I? I'll be like this black cloud to them both, a reminder of this totally disastrous holiday. So much for me having these brilliant, miles-better-than-Marisa new friends . . . What a joke!

And how mortifying is it that Wanda saw me mess up so badly? I don't know how I can face her, after she saw me drunk and wobbling around and not knowing what to do. Does she think I'm an idiot? I bet she does. I bet she thinks I was acting all cocky and showing off with my older friends!

Worst of all is knowing I've made Mum and Dad so worried and upset. They're never going to trust me again, are they? I bet the firefighters told them there were beer cans in the Games Room. They're going to be so angry with me for drinking!

And will the farmer make them pay for the damage?! Arghhh . . . I hadn't thought of that!

All I wanted was to have a bit of fun this evening, and now I want to just curl up and disappear. Or rewind time and say no thanks to meeting up with the twins tonight. Or rewind all the way back to last week, when everything was boringly normal and fine for our family.

Before Wanda came.

WANDA

"I'd really like to check you over, Wanda . . ."

The man who is sitting on the edge of my bed has a gentle, low voice. Maybe a Nigerian accent? He sounds a bit like Obi, who ran a youth hostel that me and Patti stayed in once in Holland. I've been listening to him for a while now, saying the same thing in slightly different ways.

"I'm fine," I mumble from inside the cocoon of my cloud duvet, with only my mouth and nose visible so I can breathe. I've said I'm fine to him a bunch of times now, but he doesn't seem up for leaving me alone.

"Wanda, I really think you should let the paramedic take a—"

"I'm FINE," I say a bit more insistently to my dad,

wherever he is in the room. "I just want to go to sleep."

I've been bundled inside my cocoon for a while; I don't know how long for. My brain's turned to mush and I don't know if I've been here for ten minutes or two hours. All I know is that I snuck into my bedroom (and my cocoon) while no one was looking. While no one was looking for *me*.

I guess Dad remembered me as an afterthought, once Margot and Charlie were seen to and taken care of. Or maybe one of the other holidaymakers said, "Wasn't there another kid with you . . .?"

But it's silly to think Dad and Gill *totally* forgot about me in the chaos of everything. When I was flopped on the grass, just after I'd stumbled out of the barn with the others, I'd turned my head and saw Dad and Gill scoop Charlie up in the BIGGEST of hugs, demanding to know what he was doing up there. Then I heard Charlie telling them in his sweet foghorn of a voice that he'd woken up and seen me sneak out of the bedroom, so he followed me to see where I was going. I'd noticed Gill do that sharp intake of breath that she does. To her, it was just another example that I was putting Charlie in danger, wasn't it?

That's when I quietly got up and walked away between the gathered, chattering grown-ups, unseen. Like a ghost.

I feel the bed bounce up. The paramedic has slipped off the bed and must be kneeling down in front of me.

"Hey, Wanda, how about you just let me take your temperature and check your oxygen levels?" I hear him suggest. "All I'd need is to scan your forehead with the temperature monitor and clip an oximeter on your finger. And if those look all right, we'll let you sleep. Would that be okay?"

I don't remember seeing anything about oximeters in the old *Your Health Manual* that I read cover-to-cover in Portugal. But maybe I missed that bit, or maybe they didn't have oximeters in 1972.

"Okay," I mumble, sticking one hand out of the cocoon, and allowing the paramedic to move the duvet back a little, so that my forehead is exposed. I look the man in the eyes. He looks as kind and concerned as his voice.

"Let's do this," he says cheerfully, clipping what feels like a plastic clothes peg to my finger and swooping my forehead with a laser gadget.

"Are you feeling breathless at all, Wanda?" he asks, as he makes a note of my stats.

"No," I tell him.

(I do feel breathless.)

"And are you in pain anywhere?" he checks.

"No," I reply.

(My feet hurt so bad.)

In the background I hear Charlie calling out from somewhere else in the cottage and then Dad apologising and saying he'd better go check on him.

"Sure," the paramedic says to Dad, before turning back to me. "Your vitals look good, Wanda. You've probably had a bit of a shock and just need to rest and process it. Will I tell your dad you're fine and that you're going to sleep now?"

"Yes please," I mumble, and smile weakly.

(I'm not going to sleep for a single second tonight . . .)

WEDNESDAY

MARGOT

OMG, Diary,

Wanda's gone.

I don't know where; it's still kind of early – 7am – but she's definitely gone. Her duvet is pulled up all neat and her gran's photo and her teddy and her rainbow bag are missing, which means she is too.

I only found out cos Charlie shook me awake and he was crying and saying something about how he had a nightmare about the fire and came through to sleep on Wanda's bed again, only she wasn't there.

And now Mum's freaking out and Dad's already out looking for Wanda in the fields and Pops is here and on his phone and I don't know what's happening but I know a lot of it is my fault.

IT'S ALL MY FAULT.

I know it is, because I know Wanda read some of what I wrote here. Last night, after all the drama, I went to bed in the dark so that I didn't wake Wanda. But when Charlie came bursting into the room this morning, I saw my diary lying open on the duvet down by my feet – not safely tucked under my pillow like usual.

If it was any other time, any normal time, I'd be furious at Wanda for doing that, but right now I'm more mad at myself. I cared too much about what everyone else thought, like Esha and Sam! And I was angry with Marisa for ditching me and for Pops not thinking of me as his granddaughter and I was jealous of Wanda getting to know Dad (her biological dad and not mine!) and I was even jealous of how much my stupid darling mongoose of a brother likes Wanda and I felt MORE pushed out of the family than I usually do so, yeah, I took all of that out on her.

Like, I know it's important to look after yourself and own your own feelings but I didn't take time to properly wonder what WANDA was feeling and that is so not fair, cos she's only twelve and she was here all by herself and I'm supposed to be her family, her big sister. I'm supposed to be a big sister who looks after her kid sister and I FAILED!!

I mean, last night SHE looked out for ME, but everyone was in a state and everything got muddled and emotional after the fire and . . . and she's gone!

Where is she? WHERE IN THE WORLD IS WANDA?????

#PleaseLetHerBeAlright
#PleaseLetHerBeAlright
#PleaseLetHerBeAlright

WANDA

The train station didn't seem that far away when I saw the symbol for it on the sat nav in Dad's car on Monday, or when we passed it in real life on the way to buy nit shampoo in the pharmacy in town yesterday.

But when it's super early in the morning and more shivery-cold than you'd expect in summer, and when your feet hurt cos they got a bit blistered in the fire, it's quite a long way to walk.

And it's so weird to be sitting on a platform with no one around. Sort of spooky, even though the sun is shining.

BLING-BLEEP-BLING! goes an alert from a loudspeaker, making me jump.

A loud recorded voice announces that a train is arriving. Not mine, annoyingly; it's one going in the opposite direction, and it's already appearing around the bend and swooping towards the platform opposite and grinding to a halt.

I wish my train would hurry up. I just want to get away from here now. Dad and Gill – or more likely Mr Swanson – are probably getting in touch with social services right now, while they think I'm still asleep. Organising the best way to get rid of me and start again without Wanda-The-Annoying mucking things up for them.

I check the noticeboard overhead – my train is still ten long minutes away. Which gives me plenty of time to gaze down at the ticket in my hand again. I got it out of a machine by the entrance. I used the bank card Gran gave me before she died, panicking that it might not work for some reason, or that I'd forget the PIN for it, but of course I hadn't, since all that time ago Gran made me practise it so much that it's like the number is printed onto the inside of my eyelids.

I can't help glancing up as the train begins to

move off, curious to see who'd got off at this middle-of-nowhere station. The only passengers seem to be a mum with a little kid and a baby strapped to her chest. The mum suddenly waves and smiles over in my sort of direction . . .

"Yoo-hoo, hello, Jaya, darling!" a voice calls out quite close to me, and I turn to see an older lady in a bright red tunic with a big smile on her face.

"Hello, Nani!" the little kid calls back, before running towards the metal staircase and bridge that'll take her over to this side of the track and her grandmother's waiting arms.

Watching this cute scene, my breath sort of gets sucked out of my chest.

To be loved. To be wanted. What must that feel like?

What if my own gorgeous gran hadn't died? Would everything have been different? Would Patti still have wanted to go travelling? Would she have wanted to take me with her, or would it have been a lot easier for my mum if she knew she could leave me behind to live with Gran? Instead of me holding her back?

But what's the point of thinking like that, I tell myself, sniffing a bit and wiping my nose and eyes with the bottom of my Nirvana T-shirt. I've just got to keep moving forward.

Forward. Don't look back. Just look down again – AGAIN! – at the ticket in my hand and talk myself through the plan.

Okay, so . . .

1) I've got to change somewhere I've never heard of.
2) Then I'll get to Dover.
3) After that, I'll have to find my way from Dover train station to the ferry terminal. Easy, right?

Uh-oh – here come the hamster wheels of doom . . .

- What if I forget to get off at the place I've never heard of?
- What if the train I get on doesn't even STOP at the place I've never heard of, and I end up going to London or Edinburgh or another place I've heard of by mistake?

- And IF I manage to get to Dover, what do I do then?
- Is the train station far from the ferry terminal?
- I hope it isn't far. My feet are too sore to walk much more.
- Is there a bus I need to take?
- Where will I get a bus from?
- How much will a bus cost? £1.50? £15? £50?
- Do I have that much in my bank account?
- And if I've got enough in my bank account, how do I buy an actual ticket for the ferry?
- Do I need to use the Euros I have?
- But then, are you actually allowed on a ferry if you're not in an actual car?
- Can you just walk right on?
- Or will someone try to stop me?
- Will they stop me because I'm not in a car, or because I'm twelve and need an adult with me?
- What happens when I get to France?
- I HAVEN'T THOUGHT WHAT I'LL DO WHEN I GET BACK TO FRANCE!!
- How will I get to the eco-farm?
- Will Patti even be there, or will she have seen

her chance and taken off somewhere exciting with Jakub?

- But she WILL be there, won't she?
- Patti does really care, doesn't she?
- And if she doesn't, what will I—

BLING-BLEEP-BLING! The questions and the worries growling and grinding in my mind stall at the sound.

And no, it's STILL not my train. The announcer is yabbering on about yet *another* train arriving on the other platform.

I drop my head in my hands, but that doesn't help. With my eyes shut, I just picture the loveliness of going on holiday with my new family, then the spikiness and disaster of yesterday. You know, I thought Mr Swanson was a bad omen when he turned up at Badgers Bottom. But I'M the bad omen. I'M THE BAD OMEN! Even if things weren't totally fine in my dad's family, they were still pretty good. Till I turned up and turned everything upside down.

And I'm like a firestarter, with actual real fires

happening all around me, and then I've just set a bonfire under my new family, making them all unsettled and unhappy and—

"WANDA!"

The train on the opposite platform has just started up again and rumbled off to the next station.

Only one person seems to have disembarked this time. Someone with a crown of blonde dreadlocks, a worried expression and a smile a mile wide.

"WANDA!! BABYCAKES!!"

One second my mum is standing there – two electrified railway tracks away from me – and then she is running towards the stairs and bridge that will bring her over to my side. I watch her come; she's on the phone to someone, she's waving madly, her chunky necklaces bouncing off her chest as her sandals tip-tap down the stairs on this side of the track and then I'm running towards her and I'm in her arms and I smell sunshine and France and the geranium-scented perfume she always wears.

Patti. My mum. Us. Just us, like it's always been.

"Why are you here?" I snuffle into her T-shirt. "It's only Tuesday!!"

"What?" Mum laughs, pushing me away just enough for her to still hug me but for her pale-blue eyes to take in my whole, tear-soaked face.

"You . . . you were meant to be at the retreat till Saturday! I thought you wouldn't get my messages till then at least!"

"Well, Sweetpea," says Patti, smoothing my hair from my face, the way she's always done since I was little. "It was as if the stars aligned and everything made sense and—"

"Nope," I interrupt her, smiling but shaking my head. "Don't give me stars, Patti. Tell me something real!"

"Well, what I mean is, I meditated about our situation and next steps, and then what I realised was, well, that I was an idiot to leave you, darling! So I quit early, and collected my phone from the reception yesterday evening, and when I switched it on, there were ALL these messages about you!"

"Huh?" I say, confused. "But I only left you two messages! One to say where I was going, and then one on Monday saying—"

"Saying you were having the best time and not to come for you, right?" Patti laughs. "So yes, there were your messages. Then there were a bunch from your dad, since you'd given him my number . . ."

I nod, thinking how weird it must've been for Patti to hear Lee's voice after all these years.

". . . and then Hélène tracked me down, because Elif had called her and told her what had happened because she was worried about you. And then this message came through at the reception at the retreat, just as I was getting ready to leave – it was from your grandfather, Paul. He'd been trying every meditation centre he could find. I think the one I was at was the eighth one he'd contacted! He'd left a phone number that I called straight away. He sounded so lovely and so concerned about you."

"Mr Swanson?" I say.

"Mr Swanson?! That's a very formal way of referring to him!" my mum laughs. "Paul and I have been talking all through the night, while I was on the train to Calais and while I was on the ferry . . . he's supposed to be picking me up from this station to take me to you."

I blink at my mum, trying to take her in, trying to take in all her news.

"So the *real* question is, what are you doing here, Wanda?" she asks.

"You know why; I came to find my dad," I say bluntly. "Why didn't you tell me more about him, Patti? Why did you keep him secret?"

"Listen, I was going to tell you more one day, Wanda, but I thought it was more important for you to grow up just being YOU for a while," she says, with a frown. "To really be *sure* of yourself before you worried about who he was. I mean, Lee might not have been the same lovely boy I knew. He could've let you down, and I didn't want that for you."

I could've said right then that *she'd* let me down at times . . .

"But we can talk more about that later, Sweetpea," she says, rubbing my arms. "What I meant was, what are you doing here, right now, all on your own at this station?"

My head swirls as I think about how to reply. Up till a minute ago, I'd've said I was running away. Running away because I was so alone, and no one cared. But now it sounds like maybe quite a lot of people cared . . .?

I feel properly shaky all of a sudden, like there are seismic tremors under my feet, as if every second of the last few days is catching up with me and shaking me from the inside out.

I feel like I might cry and cry, and that my legs won't hold me.

And then there's another pair of arms around me and Mr Swanson is lifting me up and saying, "Now, now, Wanda, dear! You're all right. You're all right. I've got you."

I open my eyes and over his shoulders I see a glint of ginger hair and Margot's sunshine smile.

I'm in a station in the middle of nowhere, but I think I might be home.

Home.

SEPTEMBER

WANDA

'Wow, big day! You'll smash it, Wanda!! See you tonight for celebratory PIZZA. Dad x'

It's 8am and Dad's already at work, at the hospital. I text him back a thumbs-up, a smiley face and a pizza, plus a cactus, moose and boomerang too, because . . . why not.

So, school . . .

I have to go to school today. Gulp.

I'll have to remember which maze of corridors each of my classrooms are in and what all the teachers are called and where the loos are and where I'm meant to leave my packed lunch and about a million other New Girl stuff.

At least I'm not the *only* New Girl.

"Are you all set, Wanda?" Patti asks, smiling at me from the kitchen table.

"No," I semi-joke, as I check I've got my pencil case for the forty-twelfth time. "Are *you*?"

"No, not at all!" says Patti, laughing as she pushes the chair back and stands up. "Sorry for dropping in without notice, Gill! And thanks for the coffee!"

"No problem, Patti! Any time!" Gill calls through from the hall, where she's helping Charlie into his sweatshirt. As I've come to know all too well, trying to help Charlie get dressed is like trying to wrestle an octopus into a babygrow.

So, yeah, while I'm starting in Year 8 at secondary school today (eek!), Patti is starting her new job helping refugees learn English at a centre in town. She's saving up for a flat that's big enough for the two of us, but that might take a while. It's okay though; I'm fine here at Dad's. Me and Margot and Mr S have done a TON of DIY this summer; we painted the garage walls white and put together a bunch of flatpack furniture so it looks great as Gill's new office. Then there was more flatpack action as the airbed I was sleeping on in Gill's *old* office was swapped for this cool hi-rise bed with a desk under it, where I can do my homework (homework – eek!!). For the walls, I chose a blue like the sea and the sky, like the Greek flag. Gran's photo – and more framed family photos – are up on the shelf in my new room. Teddy Theo is up there too, along with a clay shark Charlie made for me as a moving-in present (looks more like a potato with teeth and a tail but I LOVE it, of course).

And Patti is fine for the moment, staying with Mr S, sleeping in my dad's old childhood bedroom! It's only temporary, while Patti gets herself together. My mum and grandfather might KILL each other if it was permanent! I mean, Patti and Mr S like each other a lot, but have pretty different views on a few (hundred) things . . .

It took a while to settle on what I should call my grandfather. 'Pops' felt like it was too much Margot and Charlie's thing, something special from *their* childhood, one I wasn't part of. Anyway, no matter how well me and him get on now, I'll never think 'Pops' suits someone as (sometimes) serious and stern as my grandfather! Anyway, we both settled on 'Mr S' by accident . . . he watched me scribble a note for Gill one day – *'Me & Margot out getting paint with Mr S'* – and he did this snort and smiled and said "'Mr S', eh?", and that was it. It stuck. It's like our little in-joke. And Mr S has a nickname for me too; he calls me Her Royal Highness, Wanda the Second (since his wife was technically Wanda the *First*). Yeah, he's pretty funny when he wants to be, for someone so serious and stern . . .

And Mr S is also surprisingly surprising! That time at Badgers Bottom, when I stormed up to his posh hut, with my nit-treatment hair drip-dripping and my bin-bag cape flip-flapping and lectured him about ADHD? He'd already Googled all about it. He kept trying to tell me that, but I didn't give him a second to reply. And when we were at the firepit later that day, when Mr S said it would be good to have a catch-up with me in the morning (which didn't happen, since I'd run away!) he'd actually just wanted to tell me that he'd had a good, long think about ADHD running in families. It had suddenly become *blindingly* clear to him that so many of his wife's 'quirks' matched the things I'd described. Yep, seems like Wanda the First had ADHD, same as Wanda the Second! And now *he's* the one giving *Gill* lectures about being more patient and accepting of Charlie's general, full-on Charlie-ness! (Gill's still reserving judgement on whether my kid brother does or doesn't have ADHD, but she seems a lot less stressed now when he whirlwinds around. Which feels like a mini-win.)

"Okay – I'd better go. Love you, Babycakes!" says Patti, blowing me a kiss. "Have a not-awful day!"

"You too!" I call right back.

There's a kerfoofle and more "Bye"s and some clatter-banging at the door and then everything goes quiet, meaning Gill and Charlie have headed off too.

The external quiet goes on for a few more blissful seconds . . . and then the internal noise cranks up inside my head. Oh, yes; the hamster wheels are still in action, even though I'm on ADHD meds now. They're just a whole lot less FRANTIC and MANIC. More like a chatterbox friend who just doesn't know when to shut up. (Yes, that DOES describe me too sometimes!)

And this morning's hamster wheel musings are . . .

- It's great that Patti's happy to live here in Dover, so I can be close to Dad and everyone!
- I can't believe how well she and Dad and Gill all get on. How lucky is that?
- I love that Patti's so excited by her new job.
- It'll be ace when she sorts out a flat, and I can spend half my time with her.
- It sounds just perfect.
- Perfect.
- But it might not be totally perfect . . .
- Patti's never going to last at this job, or this settled life, is she?
- And if she doesn't, what's the worst that can happen?
- She'll head off on her adventures again, just solo this time.
- I'll remind her that I've got a home here with Dad, so I'll be fine.
- And I'll tell her that I can come and join in on her adventures, as long as it's in the school holidays, and more like three weeks, not three years . . .

"You ready?" says Margot, sticking her head around the kitchen doorway.

"Uh-huh," I say unconvincingly.

Margot smiles her sunshine smile and motions me to follow her out of the house. She knows I've got a mountain to climb; I'm *miles* behind with all the subjects at school, no matter if Patti's tried to catch me up with English over the holidays and Mr S has tutored me in maths and science. She also knows I'm nervous of bullies spotting my neurodiverse-ness and giving me grief for it.

"Remember, I've got you," she says, at the front door. *"No one* messes with my little sister. Okay?"

"Okay!" I repeat, taking a deep breath, standing taller.

I'm also standing with my head held high and my chest up, since Gill took me clothes shopping a few weeks ago, which included getting me new PJs (finally!) and – wait for it – a bra (also finally!!). Cos that weird conversation in the holiday cottage, when Gill was slathering on the nit-treatment and asking me if there was anything ELSE my mum didn't believe in . . . I didn't get it at the time, but Gill had clocked the reason why the twins had laughed at me after I rescued Charlie from the pond (i.e. the wet T-shirt incident). Also, she'd spotted in my pitiful runaway/stowaway packing that I was completely bra-free. She'd wondered if Patti maybe didn't believe in supportive underwear for feminist reasons or something, I think.

But with the help of all my family – and the underwear department of the store in town – I am now loved, supported and unstoppable!

I am Her Royal Highness, Wanda II.

I am the amazing Wanda Swanson.

I AM READY FOR THE WORLD!!*

* As soon as I run back and pick up the packed lunch I forgot . . .

AUTHOR'S NOTE

Every story starts with something . . . a small nugget of an idea that noodles away in an author's mind for a while, that grows and grows as the author starts asking nosy questions like "What if *this* happened?", "What if *that* happened?". Next thing, the nugget and noodling and all the "what if?"s end up snowballing into a whole book.

So where did the nugget of 'World of Wanda' come from? Quite a major moment in my son's life, as it happens. After a pretty grotty and hard time at secondary school, my son went through an assessment and discovered he was neurodiverse. He had ADHD.

My son being neurodiverse made a lot of sense for him *and* for me and his dad. Eddy had long suspected that was the reason things had been so difficult for him at times, and it was a real relief for him to now understand himself better.

And what about me, as Eddy's mum? I was really pleased, of course, but I was annoyed with myself for not spotting earlier that my own kid had ADHD.

I mean, didn't I already know lots about the condition? Over the years, hadn't I seen traits in friends and other members of my family, and thought, "Hmm . . . ADHD?".

Here's the thing: in a nutshell, I'd always thought ADHD was about struggling to focus and being very fidgety. Talking too much, too. On the outside, my son didn't seem *anything* like that. As it turned out, all *his* chatter and fidgeting and struggles with focus were all happening *inside*, tucked away in his head. It was a very busy, stressful and chaotic environment in there, but he didn't know how to explain it, so he 'masked', i.e. hid his feelings. He'd also 'mirror' – i.e. copy – his neurotypical friends' behaviour, so it looked as if he was coping, doing just fine. As his parent, *I* had no clue about the internal tornado that was going on behind his smile. But as I came to understand, Eddy's version of ADHD is known as the 'inattentive' type.

Okay, so to get technical – well, *my* version of technical, which isn't very technical at all – there are THREE types of ADHD, which look like this . . .

• **Hyperactive:** The 'H' in ADHD. The one everyone recognises as the condition, when someone is pretty 'zoomy' in the way they act and talk. When they find it hard to concentrate and sit still.

- **Inattentive:** All of the above, but the frenzied zoomies are happening in the privacy of someone's overheating head.
- **A mix of both.**

So whichever version of ADHD people might have, what sort of things might they struggle with? Well, there are about a zillion, but let me throw just a few examples around . . . Those with ADHD can have problems with concentration, listening, following instructions, staying on task, overthinking, being too impulsive. They might talk too much, have *waaaaay* too much energy, make a ton of careless mistakes, forget stuff, lose stuff, including track of the time.

And there's more; people with ADHD can totally throw themselves into hobbies and subjects they find interesting and be absolutely brilliant at them (hyper-focus), even though they might switch off from some passion and forget it completely before throwing themselves into a new one. They can be very aware of other people's words, moods, feelings and body language (hyper-sensitive), though they have low self-esteem and aren't very good at being kind to themselves. They can also be constantly on the look-out for problems and details and dangers (hyper-vigilance), though that can be pretty tiring as well as useful.

As you can see, there's a lot of ping-ponging between extremes!

And as you can imagine, all that zooming and hyper- this-and-that can be absolutely EXHAUSTING, running the ADHDer's batteries down to zero. (You can sometimes spot them completely zoning out when you're talking to them.)

There I was, and here I still am, learning more and more about ADHD. Talking to my son so I can understand when things are tripping him up, and giving him an extra dollop of understanding when his brain is fizzing too much! And while we talk about the negative traits of ADHD – the stuff that makes life more complicated and tiring than it is for neurotypical people – we also talk about the positives. So many people thrive in their careers, because their hyper-focus, hyper-sensitivity and hyper-vigilance makes them extra creative, or extra empathetic; amazing with detail or great in pressured situations.

And speaking of careers, mine is being an author. So it felt like the right time to tell the story of Wanda, who very much has the third recognised type of ADHD, a mixture of both 'hyperactive' and 'inattentive'. I hope you enjoy her journey – from France to a new version of her family! – and perhaps get more of a feel for what it's like to have a frantic but often fabulous ADHD mind.

And while everyone's experience of ADHD is different, depending on their personal mix of symptoms, Wanda's ADHD is very much based on my son's. So of course I couldn't have written it without my special advisor, who read and commented on this story at every stage, to make sure it felt real and right to him.

Thanks for your knowledge and enthusiasm, my darling Eddy! Wanda's story is as much yours as it is mine, babes . . .

P.S. Eddy is convinced I have traits of ADHD. But, hey, that's another story . . .

IF YOU LIKED THIS, YOU'LL LOVE:

HOW TO BE A REVOLUTIONARY

Don't judge a friend by its tail

FIND YOUR PASSION
BUILD A TEAM
CHANGE THE WORLD

LUCY ANN UNWIN

SIMON PACKHAM

WORRYBOT

HAVE YOU EVER WONDERED HOW BOOKS ARE MADE?

UCLan Publishing is an award-winning independent publisher specialising in Children's and Young Adult books. Based at The University of Central Lancashire, this Preston-based publisher teaches MA Publishing students how to become industry professionals using the content and resources from its business; students are included at every stage of the publishing process and credited for the work that they contribute.

The business doesn't just help publishing students though. UCLan Publishing has supported the employability and real-life work skills for the University's Illustration, Acting, Translation, Animation, Photography, Film & TV students and many more. This is the beauty of books and stories; they fuel many other creative industries! The MA Publishing students are able to get involved from day one with the business and they acquire a behind-the-scenes experience of what it is like to work for such a reputable independent.

The MA course was awarded a Times Higher Award (2018) for Innovation in the Arts and the business, UCLan Publishing, was awarded Best Newcomer at the Independent Publishing Guild (2019) for the ethos of teaching publishing using a commercial publishing house. As the business continues to grow, so too does the student experience upon entering this dynamic Masters course.

www.uclanpublishing.com
www.uclanpublishing.com/courses/
uclanpublishing@uclan.ac.uk